"You don't gi...
woman who v...

A spark ignited deep inside. Deep where she hid her feelings behind a facade of calm composure.

"What do you want, Paul? A fiancée who bats her eyelashes at you and follows you around like an orphaned puppy, panting for attention?"

Eva feared she'd come close to that in her teenage years, using any excuse to trap him into conversation, wishing he'd see her, just once, as a desirable woman instead of someone he had to be polite to.

"Of course not!"

"Good." Her chin tilted up. "Because I don't recall you being particularly lover-like, either." Except that one time when he'd tried to kiss her. But even she, as close to a complete innocent as you could get, had realized his heart wasn't in it. He'd thought it expected of him, but there'd been no real enthusiasm.

Even now, years later, that hurt.

Maybe she should cut her losses after all. Walk away from Paul and hope, one day, to find another man who'd make her heart beat faster.

Except she couldn't. Not while she loved him. The thought of turning her back on him carved an aching hollow right through her middle.

She was trapped by her feelings. Not by public expectations or the legal documents binding them.

Growing up near the beach, **Annie West** spent lots of time observing tall, burnished lifeguards—early research! Now she spends her days fantasizing about gorgeous men and their love lives. Annie has been a reader all her life. She also loves travel, long walks, good company and great food. You can contact her at annie@annie-west.com or via PO Box 1041, Warners Bay, NSW 2282, Australia.

Books by Annie West

Harlequin Presents

Inherited for the Royal Bed
Her Forgotten Lover's Heir
The Greek's Forbidden Innocent
Demanding His Desert Queen
Revelations of a Secret Princess
Contracted to Her Greek Enemy
Claiming His Out-of-Bounds Bride

Passion in Paradise

Wedding Night Reunion in Greece

Secret Heirs of Billionaires

Sheikh's Royal Baby Revelation

Visit the Author Profile page
at Harlequin.com for more titles.

Annie West

———

THE KING'S BRIDE BY ARRANGEMENT

Recycling programs
for this product may
not exist in your area.

ISBN-13: 978-1-335-40378-0

The King's Bride by Arrangement

Harlequin Enterprises ULC
22 Adelaide St. West, 40th Floor
Toronto, Ontario M5H 4E3, Canada
www.Harlequin.com

Printed in U.S.A.

This book is for all the people who read *Revelations of a Secret Princess* and asked if King Paul would get his own story.

Thank you for your enthusiasm!

I had a wonderful time writing this. I hope you enjoy it as much as I did.

CHAPTER ONE

'PRINCESS EVA OF TARENTIA.'

The chamberlain projected his voice across the glittering crowd that filled the ballroom's gilded antechamber.

Heads turned, keen eyes sizing her up, from her brown hair, piled high, past the sapphire drop earrings to the ball gown of royal blue.

Eva felt their stares, as she always did, like hundreds of tiny pinpricks. But at twenty-four she'd learned to accept the public's interest. She no longer shrank from the limelight as she had when young.

Besides, there was only one person here whose opinion she cared about.

There he was, chatting to a blonde in silver sequins. At the chamberlain's words, he looked up to where she stood on the staircase above the throng. His mouth lifted in a smile.

Eva's heart tripped a beat then hammered faster. She felt the pulse high in her throat.

Even from this distance Paul did that to her. She was too far away to feel the full impact of those stunning indigo eyes but his smile always unravelled her. From the day at fifteen when she'd first seen him, thundering down the polo field, so athletic, so handsome and so *nice*. After the match her brother Leo, who'd been on the opposing team, had introduced them and Eva had been instantly smitten.

Because the then Prince Paul of St Ancilla hadn't thought it uncool to talk to his acquaintance's little sister. He hadn't seemed to notice her braces or the lingering spots that had erupted thanks to her monthly cycle. He'd been kind and friendly even when she'd been tongue-tied.

Eva had been in love with him ever since.

She moved down the staircase with practised grace, keeping her chin high. Woe betide any princess who couldn't descend a grand staircase without looking at her feet. Even in a full-length dress and high heels.

She reached the floor and pinned on her social smile for the St Ancillan Prime Minister, who enquired if she'd had a good journey. As the flight from Tarentia in northern Europe to the Mediterranean Island of St Ancilla wasn't long, the question was a formality. Yet Eva felt herself relax. After four years of regular visits to St Ancilla, she and the Prime Minister were well acquainted.

'Here's His Majesty now.' The Prime Minister turned and inclined his head in a bow.

Instantly Eva's smile solidified, the muscles in her cheeks stretching taut as she fought the urge to grin up into Paul's face. The inevitable rush of excitement she felt around him always undermined her and she strove not to reveal her feelings. It was never a problem with anyone else but around Paul it was a constant worry.

Because she felt so much while he felt so little.

Her heart beat an urgent tattoo and moisture glazed the back of her neck as he neared. She angled her head up to meet his gaze. Eva's breath released in a sigh of resignation as she met those amazing dark-blue eyes.

What had she expected? That absence would make the heart grow fonder? That in the months since they'd last seen each other he'd realised what a treasure she was?

That he'd developed feelings for her?

Or, impossibly, that she'd read the eager heat of desire in his face?

Deep inside, disappointment stirred.

Paul's easy smile was the same one he gave the Prime Minister. The same one he'd worn when he'd tilted his head to listen to the blonde siren in shimmery silver.

The blonde who'd defied royal protocol and stood so close to the King it was a wonder a discreet bodyguard hadn't hauled her away. Eva had noticed and had to repress a spike of unreasonable jealousy.

'Princess Eva. You look as delightful as ever.' Paul's deep voice tugged at her vulnerable heart.

He took her hand and lifted it to his mouth, and Eva fought to stop her expression betraying her. Her forehead twitched and the corners of her mouth compressed with the effort not to grin with delight.

As it was, she hoped Paul couldn't see the way her nipples hardened into needy peaks just because he touched her.

He was everything a king should be. Hard working, decent, dedicated and caring of his people. She loved all those things about him. But, even after knowing him for nine years, it was the angle of his high-cut cheekbones, the handsome line of jaw and nose and his vibrant aura of energetic, virile maleness that got to her every time. Even the way his coal-black hair had a tendency to flop over his forehead turned her insides to mush.

Reluctantly Eva tugged her hand from his, too conscious that a tiny change in his grip would reveal the too-rapid flutter of her pulse at her wrist.

She caught a glimpse of something in his eyes. Annoyance? Surprise? But of course it was gone in an instant. Royals were trained to conceal rather than reveal emotions.

It was tempting to wonder if he was disappointed at her withdrawal. But she was a pragmatist, despite her romantic feelings for him. She forced herself to face the truth. Paul might be surprised at her withdrawal but not saddened.

'Thank you, Your Majesty.' Meticulously, she used his title, as protocol demanded of their first meeting in six months. She sank to the polished floor in a deep curtsey.

'Paul, please.'

'Thank you, Paul.'

Protocol also decreed that, given their circumstances, she could address him by his first name in public, with his permission.

She bit down hard on the impulse to gush that he looked terrific himself.

The dress uniform of black, navy and gold showcased his tall, upright figure. He should have looked distant and untouchable in his regalia but instead he was mouth-wateringly attractive. Her fingers tingled with the desire to reach out and touch him. To follow the line of those wide shoulders and down across his powerful chest.

Paul didn't hold out his hand to help her rise. Why should he when she'd just tugged away from him? Yet Eva noted the fact, just as she noted the hint of a frown marring his brow.

A little shiver of premonition scrolled down her spine.

Now she stood before him, she realised his smile looked pinched. It certainly didn't reach his eyes.

'You had a good flight, despite the delay?'

What was that note in his voice? Not censure, not annoyance, but definitely something strained.

Once more Eva experienced that inching shiver of disquiet. This time it felt like a chill cascading down her vertebrae.

'Yes, it was fine.' She'd only just arrived in time to change and meet him here at the ball rather than in private. 'A mechanical problem held us up on the tarmac. But the flight itself was uneventful.'

Paul nodded. 'You're safely here. That's the main thing.'

Yet, reading his expression, Eva felt something else was going on. Something she didn't yet understand.

Not that she expected him to confide in her. They didn't have that sort of relationship, no matter how much she wished they did.

'Shall we?' He lifted one hand and, after a moment's hesitation in which she marshalled all her resources to appear cool, Eva put her hand on his.

Instantly heat rushed through her bloodstream from the point of contact and spread all through her body.

The one mercy was that Eva didn't blush. Paul and all the people around them had no idea of her body's hectic response to his touch.

He turned and they walked together across the room. The throng of guests parted to make way, men bowing and women curtseying. Eva noticed more than one woman followed Paul's progress with longing in their eyes.

Before them a pair of gigantic gilded doors was flung open onto the ballroom. The blaze of light from rows of chandeliers, reflected in a wall of mirrors, dazzled. But, as she'd been trained to do, Eva entered the room with head held high, conscious of the swell of the crowd following them.

Paul led her to a point dead-centre under the biggest and brightest of the chandeliers. They stopped on the ornate star that marked the middle of the exquisite, heritage-listed parquetry floor.

Under the brilliant light she read lines bracketing his mouth that hadn't been there six months ago. And around his eyes was a look of tension.

Impulsively, Eva squeezed his hand. 'Paul, are you—?'

'The ball will be opened,' boomed the chamberlain, 'by His Majesty King Paul of Ancilla and his fiancée, Princess Eva of Tarentia.'

Applause filled the room as every eye focused on them.

For once Eva didn't care. She leaned closer to the man before her, sure now that something was amiss.

'What is it?' she whispered. 'Something's wrong.'

For an instant his eyes widened, as if in surprise that she'd noticed, then his mouth curled up in a crooked smile that didn't look in the least amused. 'Not now, Eva. Not here. Later.'

Then King Paul, the man she'd been betrothed to for four long years, clasped her hand in his and curled his other arm around her back. Heat shimmered everywhere he touched and Eva froze, fighting hard not to respond.

For a second longer they stood, toe to toe, gazes locked, separated by the precise distance decreed by royal decorum. Then, as the music swelled, Paul swept her into a waltz with the superb grace of a natural athlete and all the warmth of an automaton.

Paul danced the last dance of the night with Karen Villiers, head of the new software company he'd lured to set up headquarters in the capital city's business park. Lured with tax incentives designed to make St Ancilla an appealing long-term investment prospect.

Right now, though, it seemed it wasn't St Ancilla that she saw as appealing. It was him.

Keeping a smile on his face, Paul put a little distance between himself and Karen's sinuously seductive body. A curvaceous blonde, she was very attractive. He hadn't missed how her minimalist silver dress showed off her spectacular body.

But he wasn't in the market for a girlfriend. Not even a dalliance, especially under the glare of public attention.

He wasn't free. He had a fiancée! Here, at the ball.

The thought of Eva tightened the iron bands clamp-

ing his skull and the dull pounding in his temples intensified.

It had been a long day, a long month, and the day
was far from over. He couldn't allow it to end without
talking to his fiancée. No matter how little he relished
the prospect.

There'd been a moment, as he'd looked up and seen
her at the head of the staircase, when he'd been glad she
was here. Not because it meant that at last they could
have the interview he'd been dreading but because it
was good to see her.

The feeling hadn't lasted.

Eva being here meant unpalatable duty, even if it
was for the best.

Then there was the way she'd reacted to him or, more
precisely, not reacted. As usual. In her teens she'd been
shy but engaging, and everything he'd heard about her
from Leo and others indicated she was warm and gen-
erous. But in adulthood—with Paul, at least—it was
another story.

To others she was charming and gracious, but with
him cool and distant. To the extent that he'd wondered
why she'd agreed to their engagement. Except he knew
the answer to that. It had been arranged by their parents
and she'd been left little choice.

It rankled that she didn't care for him. That she'd
never have chosen him for herself.

No wonder she held herself aloof. Never unfriendly,
but guarded. Distant.

Unlike the woman leaning too close in his arms.

For a moment Paul wondered what it would be like

to accept the implicit invitation in Karen Villiers's wide eyes and sultry body. And instantly stifled the thought.

Honour dictated there would be no other women while he was betrothed. Even if he and his fiancée had never got more intimate than him kissing her hand.

Fire shot to Paul's belly as the effects of four years of celibacy made themselves felt.

That was one thing that would change after tonight.

Was it any wonder he felt on edge? He was torn between the almost impossible demands of St Ancilla, and the need to preserve an illusion that all was well here, while keeping a lid on natural masculine desires. After four years of continuous strain he felt perilously close to the breaking point.

As the music reached its closing bars his gaze sought Eva. There she was, dancing with the famous film director who was here checking out locations for his next movie. Paul's staff had labelled him difficult yet the guy was laughing at something Eva had said.

A dart of something sharp pierced Paul's chest as he saw Eva's answering smile. It transformed her composed features into something altogether different.

'So, Your Majesty,' said a throaty feminine voice. 'I thought I'd end the night at the new night club everyone's talking about. Is there a chance I'll see you there?'

He looked into Karen Villiers's face and read the invitation in her saucy smile. Not just to a night club but to something far more intimate.

'I'm afraid not. I have further commitments tonight.'

Once more his gaze turned towards his fiancée, still deep in conversation with her dance partner, even though the music had ceased. Paul's brow twitched.

What did she find so fascinating about a man so famously self-absorbed? Her slim frame was tilted towards him as if she drank in his every word.

'Ah, of course. I'd forgotten Princess Eva is here now.'

Paul turned his attention back to the woman before him. Did she really think he'd lope off to a rendezvous with her, leaving his fiancée in the palace? Or that he'd been available for an affair until the Princess had arrived, as if out of sight was out of mind?

Suddenly Ms Villiers's sex appeal dimmed.

Eva might not care for him much but they understood each other and had grown up with the same values, the same sense of dedication to duty.

He supposed it was remarkable in his case, given the example of his appalling father. Yet maybe it was because of him that Paul had leaned the other way, choosing integrity over dishonesty. Plus, there had been the influence of his mother and tutors, all determined to make him the sort of ruler his father had never been.

Paul realised he was scowling and rearranged his features into a smile. 'It's kind of you to invite me. I hope you enjoy yourself. Now, if you'll excuse me, I must go.'

It took an inordinate amount of time for the ballroom to empty. Finally he was alone with his fiancée.

Eva stood, as still as one of the statues on the wide terrace outside. Only her eyes, an unremarkable smudge of colour between grey and blue, hinted that she wasn't as sanguine as she appeared.

Paul recalled her surprising hint of concern before the ball and wondered if she'd guessed his discomfort.

That would be a first. They'd never been close enough to share secrets or develop a sense of intimacy.

He drew a slow breath. He wasn't looking forward to this.

'Do you fancy a nightcap, Eva? It's been a long evening, but we need to talk.'

Did he imagine that she drew in a sharp breath? Certainly her breasts rose high beneath the shimmery fabric of her royal blue ball gown.

'Thank you. I'd like that.'

She turned and walked with him, nodding to the members of staff waiting outside the ballroom ready to come in and restore it to its usual pristine splendour. She paused before the chamberlain and the chief housekeeper, congratulating them on the success of the event and the staff's efforts tonight.

It was the sort of thing Paul usually did. And it proved how easily Eva fitted into his world. On the face of it she made the perfect partner. He had no doubt that she'd support her husband in every way she could, sharing the burdens of royalty with grace and goodwill.

His gaze snagged on the pale shoulder bared by her dress and the sweep of her slender neck up to her neat chin. Standing beside her, he was aware of her suddenly as a desirable woman rather than a life partner in a dynastic marriage neither of them had asked for.

Then she turned, caught him watching, and the remnants of her smile died.

One thing was clear. Eva didn't desire him. Sometimes he wondered if she even approved of him. Did she think he was tarred with the same brush as his dead father? Bitterness coated Paul's tongue at the thought of his old man, repugnant in so many ways and still the source of most of Paul's problems.

But he was being unfair to Eva. His fiancée might be cool and self-contained but she'd never been disapproving or disagreeable. Simply distant.

Paul gestured for her to precede him into the King's study. It had changed since his father's day, devoid now of the massive gilded desk and rows of unopened books. In their place was a modern desk, filing cabinets, framed maps of the country and a couple of comfortable lounges, which was where he led her.

'What will you have?' he asked as he un-stoppered a single malt.

'Whisky would be good, thanks. With a touch of soda.'

Paul shot a startled look at his betrothed. 'Whisky?' The most he'd ever seen her drink was a glass of wine over dinner.

Eva shrugged and once more his attention was drawn to the expanse of pearly skin left uncovered by the gown that sat off her shoulders. It wasn't revealing in the way Karen Villiers's dress had been—blatantly provocative— yet Paul felt a tangled thread of desire snarl in his belly.

Tonight Eva's air of untouchability was tempered by something else. Something deeply feminine and alluring.

As for untouchable, he recalled the feel of her in his arms, poised and regal, yet disturbingly warm and unquestionably feminine.

Four years of celibacy…

That must be the reason.

Abruptly he turned and poured two whiskies. Large ones.

Dutch courage?

He told himself this would be straightforward. Yet he had to tread carefully so as not to turn a perfectly sensible idea into a diplomatic nightmare.

'Please,' he gestured to the leather sofas, 'have a seat.'

With one last unreadable look his way, Eva subsided in a wave of royal-blue silk. The colour suited her, he decided as he leaned forward, passing her drink.

As ever she took it carefully, her fingers never touching his.

Paul jerked upright, teeth clenching. As if he needed a reminder that he wasn't her personal choice of husband! She might not say it out loud but her body language made it abundantly clear.

How on earth did she expect to get through their wedding night? By closing her eyes and thinking of her duty as a Tarentian princess?

He swung away and stalked to the window. Floodlights illuminated the perimeter of the palace gardens in the distance. A far cry from when his father had been King and they'd spent a fortune lighting up all the ornate gardens throughout the night, wasting precious energy.

'Paul? What is it? You said you'd explain. Is everything… Are you all right?'

He spun on his heel, surprised by the note of concern in Eva's voice. Or had he imagined it?

'I'm fine.' He lifted the tumbler of whisky and swallowed, letting the fiery warmth burn its way down. 'But I have something important to discuss.'

Now it came to the moment, this was more difficult

than he'd anticipated, though he was doing the right thing.

It struck him how weary he was of always doing the right thing. Of the onerous treadmill on which he ran, juggling the demands of his nation, his family and his father's creditors. For four years he'd done his best, achieved things he'd never believed possible, snatching success from the jaws of disaster. His father, dead from a massive stroke less than six months after his abdication, hadn't lived with the consequences of his actions. Nor had his mother returned to St Ancilla to support her son. Instead she lived a life of genteel retirement in Paris.

'I'm listening.' Eva was ramrod-straight, the glass cupped in her hands.

Because she feared what he might say? Yet it was Eva who'd benefit from what he must do, Paul who would pay the consequences.

He hefted a deep breath, looked down at the drink in his hands then up at his betrothed.

'I'm releasing you from our engagement, Eva. It's over.'

CHAPTER TWO

'OVER?' EVA STARED up at Paul, disbelieving her ears. Surely he didn't mean what it sounded like?

Yet the determined thrust of his chin and the tight grip of his fingers around the crystal tumbler mocked her desperate hopes. He looked like a man facing an unpalatable duty.

'You're jilting me?'

Unbelievable to discover her voice still worked. Her throat constricted and her lungs hurt. She couldn't seem to drag in enough air. Yet somehow she managed to sound utterly calm. It was as if she was listening to some other woman.

'That's a very emotional word, Eva. I'm not *abandoning* you. Just giving you your freedom.'

Her heart battered so hard against her ribs, it was a wonder he couldn't hear it.

But he looked too caught up in his own thoughts to read her emotions. His expression was severe, drawn tight with tension, disapproval or hauteur. She didn't know which. Maybe all three.

Because she'd dared to question him? That wasn't like Paul.

Eva stared up into that familiar face and felt as if the world had turned inside out.

Her fiancé was considerate and, when it came to his obligations, utterly reliable. Wasn't their engagement an obligation? He certainly didn't love her. The arrangement had been concocted for dynastic reasons but surely that meant it was even harder to break? He was a stickler for doing the right thing.

Yet Paul's expression was implacable.

She looked up at him and was torn between dismay and that old, familiar melting sensation. Because he was as heartbreakingly handsome as ever with his strongly defined features and tall, well-built frame. His dress uniform drew attention to straight shoulders and long, powerful legs, and the dark blue might have been designed to highlight his indigo eyes. Even his black hair, rumpled since he'd dragged his fingers through it, was attractive.

'Eva? Say something.'

She blinked and felt something stir inside. Something other than shock and dismay. A niggle of…anger?

'You want a response when you haven't even told me what's going on?' She stared straight back at him. 'You owe me an explanation first.'

He was lifting his glass to his mouth and stilled, arrested mid-movement.

What? Did he expect her to sit here meekly and agree to whatever he decreed? That wasn't the man she knew.

Or did he think her a complete door mat? It was true that around him she felt self-conscious, so wary of betraying her feelings that she accepted without question the arrangements made for her visits to St Ancilla. She thought that made her a good guest. It didn't mean she was a pushover.

Eva lifted her drink and downed half of it in one swallow.

She rarely drank and struggled to contain a cough as raw fire hit the back of her throat then trickled down. Seconds later warmth exploded within, counteracting the glacial chill that had crept through her inch by crackling inch at his announcement.

'I apologise.' He rubbed the back of his neck in a rare show of discomfort. 'I meant to talk with you and sort this out before the ball. But you were delayed.'

Eva felt her eyes bulge. 'What was your plan? To send me packing back to Tarentia before the ball?'

A hint of dull colour streaked across those high cheekbones.

'Of course not.' He drew himself up, the picture of frowning indignation. 'I just thought that the sooner we sorted out this situation the better, for you especially.' He shook his head. 'I thought you'd be pleased.'

Pleased!

But, of course, he had no idea how she felt about him.

She'd spent her journey to St Ancilla rehearsing how she'd persuade him that it was time to set a date for their long-delayed wedding.

While he'd been planning to sever their connection.

The irony of it made her cringe.

Suddenly Eva could no longer meet his probing gaze. She looked down to where she cradled the finely cut crystal. Colours winked as her hands trembled and the glass caught the light, a contrast to the deep blue lustre of her new gown.

It struck Eva that her dress was the same colour as Paul's eyes. Had she subconsciously chosen it for that very reason?

Her breath hitched so hard, the bodice of her strapless gown felt too tight.

Was she really so pathetic?

Grimly she took another swallow of whisky, enjoying the shocking blast of alcohol, as if it could burn away her feelings for him. Because they made her weak.

But no amount of spirits could eradicate her feelings. Something like despair hit and she slumped back in her seat.

'Why don't you just explain what's going on?'

Paul watched her warily. For the first time in years he could see the ripple of Eva's emotions just below the surface of her composure.

Yet she was still an enigma. Still unreadable. Except that now he sensed far more than her usual cool acceptance. Something stronger motivated his fiancée.

That look she'd sent him when she'd demanded an explanation! It had had all the hauteur of his father at his most uppity. And, far from appearing chilly or remote, those brilliant eyes had seared him. He'd almost swear that stare had left scorch marks.

Now, though, Eva seemed to have deflated. Her shoulders hunched in a way that aroused his protective instincts. Which was crazy. He was doing this for her.

'I know you don't want to marry me, Eva. I've known it almost from the first.'

That yanked her gaze up from her glass.

How had he ever thought her eyes a dull sort of colour? They shone with a silvery light he'd never noticed before.

'Go on,' she urged.

Paul raised his glass to his mouth, found it empty and stood.

'I'll have another too, please.' Eva extended her arm, watching him with a look that on anyone else he'd cate-gorise as challenging. When he reached out and took her glass their fingers brushed. Did he imagine her flicker of reaction? A tiny shiver?

He turned away to get their drinks, forcing his thoughts back to the issue under discussion rather than imagining Eva responding to his touch.

'You were going to explain.' Her voice gave nothing away. She might have spoken of the weather in those same polished tones.

'I thought you'd be happy,' he murmured as he topped up their drinks and turned, only to halt abruptly as he took in the sight of her.

He couldn't describe how she looked different, yet she did. More vibrant. More arresting.

He'd seen her wearing a ball gown before so it wasn't the spill of rich blue silk pooling around her feet, or the slope of pale flesh rising from it that made him stare. She wore gems but that wasn't new. Nor was the per-fect posture. It was something around her eyes and her mouth, and even about the way her breasts pressed high against the confines of her bodice. There was challenge in that brilliant stare and something more. Something almost haunted.

Could it be...*hurt*?

His chest tightened. His brows angled down in a frown as he tried to puzzle out what Eva felt.

'Happy that after a four-year betrothal you want to set me aside like an outdated fashion accessory?' Eva lifted one eyebrow in an expression he'd never seen her wear.

Okay. Not hurt then. *Angry.*

Paul leaned across and held out her glass. Once more their fingers brushed. She didn't seem to notice but he did. A spark of something like electricity tingled through his hand and up his arm. His breath stilled as he frowned down at her.

'What?' She looked up at him. 'You didn't expect me to mind?'

He shook his head and sank onto the lounge opposite her, carefully placing his glass on a side table while he sought the right words. This interview had morphed from just difficult to difficult and surprising. He needed his wits about him.

'Have you fallen in love? Is that it?' Her words whipped his gaze back to her. They snapped out, sharp and precise with an undercurrent rich in disapproval. 'Perhaps with Ms Villiers?'

'No and no.' Paul shook his head.

When would he have time to fall in love? He was too busy propping up a kingdom, working sixteen-hour days most of the time.

'Are you sure? The pair of you seemed very close tonight.'

In another woman he'd have read that tone as jealousy. But this was Eva, the woman who if anything shrank from his touch, and who'd turned away the only time he'd tried to kiss her.

'I'm King. You know a love match doesn't enter into it.'

Especially a king grappling with such financial problems. Maybe his younger brothers, currently studying overseas, might one day have the freedom to marry where they chose.

Eva sipped her drink, regarding him thoughtfully, her mouth no longer prim as usual but almost pouting, the contours of her lips glistening in the lamplight. Something stirred low in Paul's belly.

'Your sister married for love.'

'Caro is different. You know she rarely even lived at court.'

Yet that hadn't saved her from their father's machinations. His plans to marry her off to a rich banker had been the least of his crimes against her. Fortunately, she'd finally found her lost daughter and happiness with Jake Maynard. Together they'd faced down the old King and had stood by Paul when he'd ascended the throne. Now he counted his half-sister and her husband as two of his closest friends, even if they lived on the other side of the world. As far as he knew, Caro was the only member of the St Ancillan royal family to marry for love, not duty.

'So you're not in love.' Eva's tone expressed doubt. 'Then why end our engagement?'

Once more Paul heard a hint of something in her voice that might have been hurt. Except that glittering stare looked more annoyed than anything.

'For your sake, Eva.'

'Mine? It doesn't feel like it from where I'm sitting.'

Paul raked his hand through his hair then leaned forward, resting his elbows on his thighs. This conversation hadn't gone the way he'd planned. He was used to taking charge, to persuading or occasionally ordering others into acting in his country's best interests. He sweet-talked investors and handled difficult negotiations as a matter of course. But tonight, confronted with Eva, who seemed suddenly not like the Eva he knew, he'd inadvertently relinquished control.

'It's simple.' He held her gaze and watched her glass stop on the way to those lush lips. 'I know you didn't have a choice in this engagement. That you don't want to marry me. I want to give you your freedom. I don't want an unwilling wife.'

She said nothing, just looked down at her glass with a puckered brow, as if surprised to see it in her hand.

It wasn't the response he'd expected.

'Eva?'

She looked up and for a moment he read confusion in her stormy eyes. Then she looked down again at the tumbler, raised it and took a long swallow. This time she barely shuddered at the strong liquor.

'Why now? Why not refuse four years ago?'

'Because I didn't know initially how little you wanted this match. And...' He paused, the result of a lifetime's training in keeping unpalatable truths hidden. 'Soon after our engagement was announced, I discovered my father had already squandered the portion of your dowry that was transferred on our betrothal. I wasn't in a position to pay it back.'

Did she stiffen? The gems at her ears caught the light as they swayed.

'Ah. So we *are* speaking plainly.'

'I thought that's what you wanted.'

Not if it means you dumping me.

Eva bit her bottom lip rather than blurt out that home truth.

She didn't know if she should feel proud or pathetic that she had to ask. 'So you don't need my dowry any more?'

That made him sit straighter. His shoulders drew back like a soldier on parade.

What? Had she insulted him? He was the one who wanted plain speaking.

'Public funds are still tight in St Ancilla. But that's not the key issue.'

'Isn't it?'

She recalled her father's fury when he'd discovered, too late, the enormous ocean of debt the previous King of St Ancilla had run up. It was a secret known only to a select few. The two monarchs had earlier concocted a dynastic betrothal between Eva and Paul. It had come as a shock when King Hugo had abdicated soon after and retired to a distant island. A nastier shock when Eva's father had learned Hugo had been secretly forced to abdicate, then had been banished, the alternative being to have stood trial on multiple counts of fraud, theft and embezzlement of public funds.

Eva's father had wanted to cancel her engagement on the spot, but had been persuaded to let it stand rather than court unwanted media speculation. The portion of her dowry given to St Ancilla on her betrothal was long gone and she knew Paul fought to save his country from bankruptcy and scandal. From what her father had said, it would take years to make good the money stolen by King Hugo.

Even so, she'd wanted the marriage. She'd persuaded her parents to allow a long engagement, ostensibly because she and Paul were young, and so she could complete her university studies. Her parents hoped that after all this time she'd agree to end the engagement. It would surprise no one, they said, if she and Paul had grown apart over four years. That, of course, was code for the fact that there would be minimal public scandal now. Yet Eva's plan was still to marry the one man she'd ever loved. Hoping that one day he'd come to care for her the way she cared for him.

Tonight's bombshell threatened that dream.

Once more Paul forked his fingers through his hair in a gesture of frustration.

'The financial situation is getting better. Slowly.' He shook his head. 'You don't need to hear the details, Eva. The fact is I don't want your money. It would be wrong. I intend to pay back every penny.'

'You're not very like your father, are you?' She'd never liked King Hugo, an overbearing, arrogant man, far too easy to anger.

Paul's mouth curled up in a tight smile. 'Thank you. I can't think of a better compliment.'

'You're honourable.'

His dark eyebrows twitched together. 'Why doesn't that sound like a positive when you say it?'

She blinked and let her eyes widen. 'I can't imagine. It's one of the things I like about you.'

'You do? I didn't think you liked me at all.'

'You think I'd promise to marry a man I don't even like?' He really did think her a door mat!

He shrugged those lovely broad shoulders but Eva kept her eyes on his. 'My father was a master in the art of coercion and bullying. I thought…'

'That mine is too?' She shook her head. 'He's proud and stiff-necked but he's no bully.'

It was only when Eva had shyly admitted to her parents that she wanted to marry the Crown Prince of St Ancilla that the betrothal had gone ahead.

Her mistake, apparently, had been not telling Paul himself. Because she feared he'd read her true feelings and be scared off by a clinging wife. Because he'd never been interested in her romantically. From what she'd heard and observed as a teenager, his taste ran to well-endowed blondes. Since their engagement, there'd mercifully been no gossip about him with any woman other than her.

She drew a fortifying breath. 'My parents never forced my hand, Paul. I was content to marry you. I still am.'

'Content?' His mouth twisted in a grimace but even now he was the most attractive man she'd ever known.

'Happy, then. I'm happy to marry you.'

'You don't give the impression of a woman who wants to marry me.'

A spark ignited deep inside. Deep where she hid her feelings behind a façade of calm composure.

'What do you want, Paul? A fiancée who bats her

eyelashes at you and follows you around like an orphaned puppy panting for attention?'

Eva feared she'd come close to that in her teenage
years, using any excuse to trap him into conversation,
wishing he'd see her, just once, as a desirable woman
instead of someone he had to be polite to.

'Of course not!'

'Good.' Her chin tilted up. 'Because I don't recall
you being particularly lover-like either.' Except that one
time when he'd tried to kiss her. But, even she, as close
to a complete innocent as you could get, had realised
his heart wasn't in it. He'd thought it expected of him,
but there'd been no real enthusiasm.

Even now, years later, that hurt.

Maybe, after all, she should cut her losses. Walk
away from Paul and hope, one day, to find another man
who'd make her heart beat faster.

Except she couldn't. Not while she loved him. The
thought of turning her back on him carved an aching
hollow right through her middle.

She was trapped by her feelings. Not by public expectations or the legal documents binding them.

'Eva? Are you all right?'

It was the first time Paul had spoken to her like that,
his voice gentle and…concerned. As if he really did care
about her feelings, not about doing the honourable thing.

She blinked and discovered her eyes were too moist.
Hastily she looked down at the glass in her hand, the
amber liquid swirling in the bottom.

'Well, if we're going to be honest, I'm not sure. Why
end the engagement now? If there's someone else, or if
you've taken me in dislike—'

'Of course I haven't taken you in dislike. You're everything I could look for in a royal bride.'

But not in a wife.

There was a difference and, innocent though she might be when it came to sex, Eva was quick to understand it. A royal bride would fulfil her regal duties, something Eva had been trained to do from birth. But a wife…a wife would share his whole life, his love, his dreams…

'And there's no one else.' He paused, his features taut. 'But it's been four years since our engagement. Time to release you. You and your family didn't know the mess St Ancilla was in when you agreed to marry me.'

He laughed, a bitter, grating sound that made him sound a decade older. It reinforced what she'd seen for herself, how the burden of the last four years had made him stronger and tougher than the glamorous young man she'd first met. '*I* didn't know, for that matter. It's not fair to tie you to me and hold you to your promise. You were only twenty when we got engaged, after all, and your father wanted you to finish your degree before we married. If we separate now, people will assume we've simply drifted apart. This way you won't be dogged by scandal.'

Eva was hurt and angry. Her pride was battered, and her self-esteem, for putting herself in this position. For cleaving to a man who patently didn't want to be tied to her. Even so, her heart turned over at his words. He didn't love her but he wanted what he believed was best for her. Even though parting ways would deny him the rest of the fortune she'd bring into the marriage.

He was noble. Self-sacrificing. Determined to set her free.

Eva didn't know in this moment whether she loved Paul of St Ancilla or hated him.

Because he'd never looked and really seen *her*. The woman behind the royal façade. The woman eating her heart out for him.

She downed the last of her drink in a defiant gulp and shot to her feet, buoyed by a sudden upswing of rebellious energy.

'Eva? What's wrong?' He stood before her, his brow creasing in a frown, and now his concern was like a match thrown on petrol.

That he had to ask showed how little he understood her.

It was on the tip of her tongue to lay it all out for him. Her feelings…how she'd pined for him for nine long years. How her schoolgirl crush had morphed into something stronger and deeper. Her determination to stand by his side, no matter how difficult the challenges they faced, to be the perfect supportive Queen through thick and thin. Her love for him.

But he wouldn't thank her. He would just be horrified.

And she'd regret it when he looked at her with pity in those stunning blue eyes.

'It's been a very long day,' she said through a throat that seemed lined with jagged glass. 'Can we continue this tomorrow?'

'It would be better to sort it out now.' He paused, his gaze probing, as if seeing the chinks in her armour. Eva stood straighter, willing the tumbling whirl of emotions back behind her tattered veneer of composure.

Finally, Paul nodded, though she read his reluctance. 'But if you're tired we can talk in the morning.'

Was it imagination or did she hear relief mixed with his impatience?

'I'll have my secretary arrange a time.'

'Of course you will.'

Because this was business. Not love.

He'd schedule a meeting and they'd sit on opposite sides of his desk while he told her again that he didn't want her.

Eva's mouth trembled as a great, welling surge of despair rose. She battened it down and swung away in a swirl of royal blue before her control slipped. 'Till tomorrow, then.'

Eva stripped off her ball gown and placed it on a hanger. Despite her fizzing temper, and the cloud of gloom around her, she'd no more think of dropping her clothes on the floor than she'd walk naked in public. Responsibility was ingrained. Royal standards had been drilled into her. From being gracious to others, standing patiently for hours in interminably long public gatherings, down to looking after the exquisite clothes she was lucky enough to wear.

Even if the sight of this gown, the same colour as her fiancé's eyes, made her want to fling it across the room and stomp on it.

It was no good. She couldn't find calm.

Because, somewhere between Paul's announcement

that he was setting her free and her escaping to her room, her heart had broken.

Hands on hips, Eva bent double, her lungs cramping at the sudden shaft of pain shearing through her chest.

Surely it should make some sound—all her dreams shattering?

Yet there was only silence, unless she counted the raw grating of her laboured breaths. Even the ripping ache behind her ribs was deathly silent.

Summoning her strength, she stood straight, to be confronted by the sight of herself in the full-length mirror. Her hair was still piled high and sapphire earrings caught the light. Yet in a nude strapless bra and panties, and equally nude stockings, she didn't look royal. Or special. Or in any way likely to capture Paul's interest.

From her mid-brown hair and indeterminate-coloured eyes to her average body, she was completely ordinary.

She sucked in a deep breath and her breasts swelled against her bra. Even then they succeeded only in looking average. Not bounteous. She knew he liked bounteous. The way he'd smiled down at Karen Villiers tonight—she of the perfectly sculpted body and pert, prominent breasts—hadn't been anything like the way he looked at her, his fiancée.

Ex-fiancée by morning.

Another breath-stealing cramp hit her and she had to concentrate on breathing through the pain.

Numbly, she pondered how a broken heart could be so painful. This wasn't just sorrow. This was physical as well as mental and emotional.

Because she'd never suffered and then got over puppy

love. Because when her friends had been going through the thrills and pangs of teen crushes she'd had none. She'd been the last of them to discover romance, and when she had, at fifteen, her feelings for Paul had taken permanent root.

Look where that had got her.

She *was* no better than a door mat. Too terrified of rejection to reveal her feelings to her fiancé and now it was too late.

Eva tilted her head, surveying her reflection. She might be ordinary but she wasn't a troll. Some men would think her attractive.

Wouldn't they?

She wrapped her arms around herself, hugging in the welling hurt, refusing to let the tears prickling her eyes gather and fall.

Somewhere out there was a man who'd appreciate her for herself. Not for the value of her dowry, or to strengthen dynastic links or to avoid a scandal. Her lip curled. That was what Paul was afraid of—stirring too much press attention that might lead to someone discovering the real reason his father had abdicated. That was why he'd waited four whole years to jilt her. Four years in which she'd spun fruitless fantasies of happy-ever-after.

Eva swung away, heart hammering. She wouldn't think of Paul. Tomorrow he'd end their engagement and she'd still love him. The thought threatened to swallow her whole.

Perhaps it was the two glasses of whisky she'd had on top of earlier champagne. Or simply that she'd reached the limit of her endurance. But abruptly Eva was overwhelmed by the need to prove she wasn't just a princess but a woman.

A desirable woman.

Pride, ego, self-respect and years of patiently waiting for Paul to notice her fused into fierce determination.

To be herself. To unwind. Not to worry about appearances or protocol. To laugh when she wanted to, talk with whomever she wanted. To go dancing, flirt with a handsome man. To live a little. To feel attractive and appreciated.

Just a few hours incognito. How could it hurt?

CHAPTER THREE

'SORRY TO BOTHER you so late, sir, but I thought you'd prefer to know. Princess Eva has gone out.'

'Out?' Paul looked at the time. Two a.m. Where would she go at this time? Never in her years of visiting St Ancilla had she made an unscheduled excursion. She'd followed the timetable devised by his staff. 'You're sure?'

Stupid question. His Head of Security would never make mistakes like that.

'Absolutely. She left via a back entrance and headed into the old town. One of my men is following at a discreet distance.'

Paul's grip on the phone tightened. The man's voice was so carefully neutral, it boded bad news. He'd been employed at the palace during King Hugo's reign and had learned discretion in the face of royals behaving badly.

Paul wanted to protest that Eva wasn't like that. There'd be no late-night gambling, drunkenness or temper displays. She'd probably just gone for a walk.

At two in the morning? When she had the whole of the palace gardens to walk in?

He remembered how she'd been an hour ago. The ripple of suppressed emotion…the look in her eyes that had haunted him since. Hurt or anger. He still couldn't catalogue it. Then her abrupt departure, leaving him to the knowledge he hadn't handled their interview well.

It wasn't a feeling he was used to. Usually he dealt with important matters far more smoothly.

But she'd been unexpectedly prickly. Not relieved, as he'd expected. Or biddable.

'Where is she?'

'At a night club.'

Paul frowned. A night club?

He couldn't imagine Eva clubbing. She seemed so… sedate. No, that made her sound priggish. It was just that he couldn't imagine her drinking and dancing in some badly lit venue to the throb of mind-numbingly loud music. Or cosying up to a stranger in the *faux* intimacy of near-darkness.

A sour taste filled his mouth.

'Is she alone?'

'Not at the moment.' His Head of Security's voice became absolutely toneless and something nasty skittered down Paul's spine. His belly clenched hard and his fingers tightened on the phone.

He opened his mouth to ask if she was with a man then shut it.

Of course she wasn't. Eva was the soul of discretion and, moreover, his fiancée.

Till tomorrow, a sly voice whispered in his ear. *From tomorrow you and she will be as good as strangers. She'll have no obligation to you nor you to her.*

Paul's mouth firmed. She was his responsibility. Not

just because of their engagement. Or because she was a
guest in his country and home, though both those factors were important.

What weighed most was the glimpse of hurt he'd
seen shadow her eyes tonight. The unfamiliar slump
of her shoulders, later banished by an almost fiercely
regal bearing that he'd sensed hid more than tiredness.

He'd taken the easy route, though, hadn't he? He
hadn't forced her to stay so they could sort out the tangle of their relationship. He'd known she was upset but
it had been easier to let her go and hope she'd have her
emotions under control by morning.

Guilt bit at his gut.

Whatever was happening, he knew Eva well enough
to understand tonight's excursion wasn't typical. Had
it been prompted by their conversation?

'Give me the location and have a car waiting for me
at the north entrance.'

Fifteen minutes later, Paul parked the anonymous
vehicle in a side street.

He'd refused a security escort but knew somewhere
behind him there'd be a minder or two discreetly melding into the night. It wasn't unheard of for royals to escape for a couple of hours' private partying. At such
times security staff kept their distance.

Paul's plan was to find Eva and bring her back to
the palace.

She had a perfect right to party but the idea of her
doing so without him, possibly prey to the advances of
predatory guys, disturbed him.

He loped down the cobble-stoned street towards the
night club, mouth tightening at the coincidence that this

was the same place Karen Villiers had invited him to.
Fervently he hoped she was no longer on the premises.

Quickening his step, he was crossing a narrow lane
on the way to the main entrance when a woman's voice
stopped him.

'I said, let *go* of me!' Gasping as if from effort,
higher pitched than normal, the voice was still familiar.

Eva.

Paul swung round and hurried towards the sound.
The lane was dark, illuminated only by a feeble bulb
near a metal door—the night club's back entrance, he
assumed. He could see movement, a jumble of figures
and a flash of light. There was a hiss of breath and a
curse.

In that moment's bright light, he saw enough. There
were people milling near the club's back door but another couple caught his attention. A woman had her
back to the wall, straining away from a man boxing her
in who pawed at her short skirt, lifting it up her thigh.

As Paul broke into a run he saw the woman jerk
one knee up and the man hunch, cursing. There was
just enough light to make out the woman's horrified
features.

Eva.

Nausea filled Paul, and an unholy rage.

He reached them as the guy straightened, filling the
air with a stream of ugly curses.

Ignoring the bystanders in the doorway, Paul grabbed
the man by the shoulder and spun him round.

It all happened so fast, Eva had trouble taking it in. A
minute ago she'd been fending off her companion's sud-

denly groping hands. She'd been stunned by how he'd morphed from debonair, amusing company to mauling octopus, his lips wet on her neck and cheek when she tried to avoid his kisses.

He hadn't taken rejection well, ignoring her first polite request that he step back. Instead he'd used his size and weight to pin her to the wall and try to lift her skirt, his other hand groping at her breast.

That was when fear had kicked in. But her desperate knee to his groin had only slowed him. Her hackles had risen in terror at what he'd said then, and the raw fury in his voice, but before he could follow through on his threats he was wrenched away.

To her right came the sound of breaking glass and the alley was plunged into darkness.

She was aware of raised voices near the club's exit but kept her eyes on the heaving figures before her. All she could discern was two men and the sound of fighting. Grunts, thuds and at one point a crunching that turned her stomach.

Then a man's voice whispered in her ear. 'Palace security, Your Highness. You need to leave now.' A hand at her elbow urged her to move away from the club.

She shook her head, trying to make out what was happening in front of her.

'We can't go. He might need help.' They couldn't abandon the man who'd rescued her.

The reply was so soft, she had to strain to hear it. 'His Majesty has things in hand. He'll join us in a moment.'

His Majesty? Did he mean Paul?

'This way, please.' She was propelled, half-carried, to the end of the alley and round the corner.

Shocked and out of breath, Eva finally gathered her thoughts and found enough purchase on the slippery cobbles to slow their progress.

'No. I refuse to go until I know he's okay.' She yanked her arm free of the bodyguard's hold, but only, she knew, because of who she was, not because she'd managed to break his grip. 'We can't just leave him. What if he's injured?'

The man opened his mouth as if to argue then stopped, turning to face the way they'd come.

Finally, over the pounding of her pulse in her ears, Eva made out the sound of footsteps approaching. She turned.

There was Paul, striding towards them. In the dim light he looked different. Bigger, somehow, and broader in a dark sweater and trousers instead of the dress uniform he'd worn earlier tonight. His hair was rumpled, falling forward across his brow, and she thought she saw a smear of something across his cheek.

'Why haven't you already gone?' He addressed the bodyguard rather than her. 'The Princess needs to be away from here.'

'The lady was concerned about you, Your Majesty.'

'Really?' Paul turned to her, his expression unreadable in the darkness.

'Really,' she said when she found her voice. 'You could have been hurt.'

'So could you.' His voice sliced like a honed blade through butter. 'Didn't you think of that?'

Eva stared up at him. She'd never heard her fiancé

angry. If anything she'd have called him even-tempered.
Yet now it sounded as if he spoke through gritted teeth.
Even in the gloom she saw the way his dark eyebrows
angled down in a disapproving V.

Was he angry with *her*?

She hadn't created that scene back there.

Abruptly she shivered, her hands rubbing her bare
arms as the night air blanketed her. But the chill in her
bones wasn't because of the weather.

'If I might suggest, Your Majesty.' The bodyguard
spoke. 'If you take the Princess away, I'll tidy up here.'

Tidy up? What did that entail?

She had to ask. 'How is he? Fabrice?'

'Fabrice?' Paul shifted closer to her.

'The man you fought.'

'You're worried about the man who assaulted you?'

*No. I'm worried about what you'll face if he's badly
injured.*

The last thing Paul needed was a scandal when every
action in his reign had been directed to protecting St
Ancilla from the revelation of his father's iniquities.
That would lead to loss of confidence in the country
and its financial system.

'If he needs a hospital—'

'Hardly. He's just a little bruised.'

Eva squinted up at her fiancé, hearing unmistakeable
satisfaction in his voice. Had he *enjoyed* the fight? The
idea was out of step with everything she knew of him.

'Okay.' Paul nodded to the security guy. 'Go and do
what needs to be done.'

'Yes, sir. And my apologies for not intervening earlier. It wasn't obvious initially that the Princess would

welcome intervention. When I realised the situation, I was delayed by onlookers.'

'I understand. I'll look after the Princess.'

Another shiver rippled through Eva. Because the man had thought she'd wanted to be groped. And because of Paul's harsh tone. As if she were some chore, an unwanted obligation.

But that was exactly what she was. Paul had just stopped pretending otherwise.

'What's so funny?'

Eva blinked and realised she'd given a huff of bitter laughter. She looked past him. They were alone now, their companion already disappearing round the corner to the lane at the back of the night club.

'Nothing.' She tilted her head higher, meeting Paul's gaze full-on. 'Absolutely nothing.'

As nights went, this was an utter disaster. The worst of her life. Rejected by the man she loved. Taken in by a charming stranger who'd offered to walk her to a taxi rank when she'd decided the night-club visit was a mistake. Groped and savagely threatened. And now, if she read the crackling atmosphere right, she'd infuriated the man who'd rescued her.

Tough. He infuriated her.

She turned away and marched down the street.

'Where are you going?'

'Back to the palace. If the police need me to make a statement, your man can direct them there.'

'There'll be no need for that.'

She tossed a look over her shoulder and found Paul right behind her, so close he could have curled his arm around her if he'd wanted. But of course he didn't want, did he? A rising tide of bitterness engulfed her.

'Why? Are you going to get your staff to paper over the incident, like your father would have done?' She stumbled to a halt, fear sucking in her breath. 'He's not going to be dumped somewhere, is he?'

Eva didn't know the full details of King Hugo's crimes but she knew he'd ruthlessly used his security services to make problems disappear. He'd had Princess Caro's infant daughter stolen from her at birth because he'd refused to acknowledge an illegitimate grandchild. Eva had been shocked when her then future sister-in-law had confided that secret, but pleased she'd trusted her with it. Especially as the story had a happy ending, Caro finally reuniting with the child she'd once believed stillborn.

'Dumped?' Paul stared down at her. 'What do you think's going on? He works for the royal family, not the Mafia.'

'Then how do you know the police won't get involved?'

He angled his head as if to view her better. 'Because I assume you don't want to press charges and face the publicity that would bring. Your Fabrice sure won't. He'll thank his lucky stars he's not locked up. Unless you *do* want the police involved?'

Eva considered it for a whole three seconds. 'No, I don't.' She cringed at the thought of reliving those horrible moments for the authorities. Of what had happened becoming fodder for the press.

What she wanted was to go back to her suite and take a long, hot shower.

'Good. Come this way.' Paul didn't touch her but gestured to a car parked up ahead, its lights blinking as he unlocked it with a remote control.

Eva didn't want to go with Paul. Didn't want to sit in that confined space with him of all people while her nerves were so jangled and her flesh crawled at the too-real memory of that man's hands on her. Especially as Paul seemed to blame her for what had happened.

'Eva?'

She glanced at those imposing shoulders, then at the solidity of that strong jaw. Why had she never thought of it as stubborn before?

She was tempted to keep on walking. To say she needed to clear her head rather than subject herself to his frowning fury. But she wasn't that stupid. She'd been gullible, trusting a stranger after such a short acquaintance, but the thought of walking down these deserted streets back to the palace…

Eva marched to where Paul stood holding the car door open. Her high heels clicked smartly on the cobbles. She kept her chin up, clutching her small shoulder bag to her side, and got into the passenger seat without once brushing against him or meeting his eyes.

Paul seethed, the satisfaction he'd got from downing the man who'd dared touch her already fading.

Her precious Fabrice.

He hadn't believed his ears when Eva had asked how he was. The man had assaulted her and yet she was concerned about him. It had been there in her voice.

Had she known him before tonight?

Was there something between them?

Paul had assumed they were virtual strangers but…

'If you take your hand away I'll shut the door.' Her voice came crisply but otherwise uninflected from inside the car.

Belatedly Paul stirred, realising he was making her a target for curious eyes with the door open and the car's interior light on. He stepped away and closed the door gently, concealing the roiling anger inside him.

No one had ever made him so furious. Except his late, unlamented father. But then King Hugo had been monstrous—narcissistic, venal and with a wrathful temper that had scorched anyone who disobeyed him.

Was it any wonder Paul had made it his life's work to contain his temper? To ensure he was as unlike his father as possible?

He shook his head and stalked round the car. Sliding inside, he shut his door and started the engine, plunging them into darkness.

But not soon enough to blot out the image of Eva's long, pale legs stretching out beside him from under that short dress.

Why hadn't he known she had legs like that? Legs that dragged a man's eyes down then up again even when his thoughts were still half with the guy he'd left sprawling in the alley. When she'd walked down the street, chin up and hips swinging… No, not walked. Sashayed. Her rump twitching, hips swaying and those legs…

Stifling a growl of frustration in the back of his throat, he reached for his seat belt and eased the car into gear.

'Buckle up.'

But of course she already had. Princess Eva of Tarentia always followed the rules. Her grasp of court etiquette was second to none, her willingness to do what was expected of her one of the reasons she'd been put forward as a royal bride.

Except when she didn't do what was expected. Like tonight.

Another thing he'd only just discovered. The fact that the woman who was still his fiancée was a rule breaker, skiving off to a night club notorious as a venue for discreet hook-ups wearing a dress that barely covered the essentials.

Then, when some chancer had tried to take advantage, had she thanked him, Paul, for rescuing her? No, she'd worried about the man who'd tried to undress her in an alleyway, all but accusing Paul of wrongdoing.

The car shot forward with a growl and the squeal of rubber on wet stone, forcing him to focus on his driving.

The way things had gone so far, he just needed to smash the car to round off a terrific evening.

Her voice cut through his turbulent thoughts. 'Are you all right?'

'I'm fine.' Belatedly he recalled she'd been concerned for him earlier. Or so she'd said. Had she been more worried about how Fabrice emerged from the encounter with Paul's fists?

'You're not acting like you are.'

Paul clenched his teeth, easing his foot off the accelerator. 'Perhaps I'm just tired. It was late when I came out to rescue you.'

Which wasn't strictly true. It had been late but he'd been wide awake, working his way through reams of paperwork. He hadn't bothered going to bed because his conversation with Eva had left him unsettled and discomfited. He wasn't used to his carefully laid plans being upended.

His mouth twisted grimly.

All these years he and so many royal advisors had considered Eva the perfect, conformable, *comfortable* royal spouse. None of them had realised her hidden, troublesome depths.

He shot her a sideways glance, caught sight of gleaming pale flesh in the darkness and registered the now-familiar grab and twist of desire low in his belly, and even lower, in his groin.

Even the sight of all that lustrous hair disturbed him. It was loose down her back and around her shoulders, and slightly dishevelled.

He couldn't help but wonder if that was how she looked in bed.

Sultry, delicious and rumpled.

He sucked in a sharp breath, trying and failing to banish the thought.

There was something subtly decadent about the sight of her hair loose, almost to her waist. It caught him on the raw that she'd worn it like that for a stranger but not for him.

Before tonight he'd felt sorry for his fiancée, trapped in a betrothal she patently didn't want. He'd worked hard not to take that personally, and had almost succeeded.

Tonight Eva had upset the tenuous balance of their relationship. Instead of sensibly agreeing to separate, she'd refused his plan. She hadn't precisely objected, but she'd tossed a spanner in the works with her announcement that she was content to marry him.

Content!

Had she any idea what an affront that was? What an insult to a man who, even allowing for the pull of his royal title, always had his fair share of female interest?

He might have inherited a kingdom that was a financial basket-case but Paul wasn't used to being dismissed so easily by any woman. He'd spent the last four years fending off females, only too eager to offer him solace and support while his fiancée was away, because he took his betrothal vow seriously.

His jaw worked and pain radiated from his grinding molars as he thought of the efforts he'd gone to for Eva. And did she appreciate them?

'This isn't the way to the palace.' Her voice came out of the darkness, drawing him back to the present.

Paul inhaled a slow breath and forced the negative thoughts to slide away. He refused to pile his frustrations one on top of the other, or to blame them all on Eva. He wasn't his father. He'd work through their difficulties and find a reasonable solution, not rage about them, lashing out indiscriminately.

'No. We passed the turn a few streets ago.'

In his peripheral vision he caught the pale oval of her face turning towards him.

'Where are we going?'

'Somewhere where we can talk without interruption.'

Because, whether Eva liked it or not, there were things they needed to sort out. Now. Tonight.

Their engagement. The potential fallout from tonight's escapade. And the unexpected zap of electric awareness between them that undercut everything he'd told himself about a lack of attraction.

He was torn between two competing impulses. To berate Eva for putting herself at the mercy of a stranger. Or pull over to the side of the road and kiss the mouth he'd discovered was anything but prim when she forgot to hold it taut. A mouth as lush and inviting as any he'd known.

Another spasm of pain circled his jaw.

One thing was certain. Tonight was a test of his control in ways he'd never expected.

CHAPTER FOUR

THE CAR PULLED up in a world of thick shadows. Tall trees lined either side of the road and they'd left the city lights far behind.

As Paul swept to a halt at the end of a long, gravelled drive, sensor lights switched on to reveal a quaint building, several storeys high, and built in a style that harked back to a previous era.

Eva blinked. It looked like some fanciful, snow-white sugar decoration. There were huge, rounded windows surrounded by whimsical plaster-work decorations, an enormous double front door, what looked like a free-form glass conservatory at one end, and at the other a tower, complete with a blue tulip-shaped dome that belonged in an illustration of some fantasy kingdom.

Her breath caught as she made out peacocks, butterflies and…was that a pair of lobsters in the intricate work beneath one window? Surely not.

'What is this place?'

Paul was already opening his door but paused. 'Welcome to the royal hunting lodge. Built by an ancestor who loved Art Nouveau.'

Eva shook her head. 'Those aren't…lobsters, are

they?' She pointed to the elaborate decoration below one window.

'They are. If you're interested, you'll also find crabs, swordfish and tortoises, along with dozens of bird species. My ancestor fancied himself as a naturalist. When he wasn't shooting the local fauna, that is.'

Amusement tinged Paul's voice and, as they sat taking in the sheer exuberance of the building before them, Eva felt a moment's bond. As if they were still friends, or at least had a common purpose.

Then, abruptly he got out, slamming the door behind him, leaving her to the sound of the engine ticking in the thickening silence.

Reluctantly Eva opened her door just before Paul got to it and swung her legs out. For a second she had the impression he was about to say something as he stood looking down at her. But his mouth turned into a thin line and he merely waited till she was out to lock the door and lead the way to the building.

'We won't be disturbed here,' he murmured as he turned on more lights and ushered her inside.

She should have known this wouldn't be like the old hunting lodges in Tarentia—closed-in spaces full of dark wood and mounted hunting trophies. The walls of the two-storey entrance foyer gleamed a soft shell-pink and a staircase, embellished with decorative ironwork that looked like butterflies in flight, curved up to the next floor.

'It's charming.'

'And costly to maintain. Unfortunately, there's a heritage listing on the building so it can't be bulldozed.'

Her head swung round at the bitterness in Paul's

voice. It wasn't something she'd heard from him before, though he carried a massive burden of responsibility, rebuilding his nation's wealth after his father's excesses.

First anger, now bitterness. What other surprises did he have for her?

He shrugged and his expression turned rueful. 'Don't worry, I'd never do it. I'm actually quite fond of the place. It's where I used to escape when...' He shook his head. 'Never mind. Come this way.'

He moved past the stairs, towards the back of the building, leaving Eva to wonder who or what he'd had to escape.

It didn't take a genius to work out it was most likely his father. But this was the first time Paul had come close to revealing any of the difficulties he'd faced as King Hugo's son. Everything Eva knew of the old King, she'd heard in confidence from her parents or from Princess Caro on a previous visit. Paul had said once he preferred not to dwell on the past but look to the future.

Because the past was so awful or because, as far as she could tell, he spent most of his time working to secure the future of his country?

'Coming, Eva?'

He stood in the shadows of the corridor, looking back over his shoulder. It struck her once more that tonight, in these casual clothes, he seemed like a stranger. Someone she barely knew.

Trepidation licked through her like a cold flame. She shrugged off the sensation and followed him.

They ended up in the kitchen. White and blue tiles and acres of scrubbed wood. It was cavernous but surprisingly cosy.

Eva had had a wrap when she'd gone to the night club but had lost it somewhere along the way. She looked down at the bare legs revealed by her higher than usual hemline and her mouth twisted. No wonder she'd felt chilled. Partly it was reaction to tonight's events and partly that she never went out wearing so little.

Maybe Paul thought the same. She looked up to find him staring at her legs from the far end of the bench where he was making hot drinks.

His stare made her want to tug her hemline down but she resisted it. There was nothing particularly skimpy about what she wore, especially compared with what she'd seen at the night club. When she stood the hem went halfway down her thighs. It was just when she sat...

'Are you warm enough?' His voice hit a gravel note.

'I'm fine.'

His gaze skated her shoulders, bare but for thin straps of satin.

Heat churned in her middle, embarrassment rising. There was no way Paul could know this wasn't actually a dress but a custom-made slip. It had been designed to be worn under a sheer chiffon dress that floated all the way to her knees like most of her other outfits. Worn separately, it looked like a plain but well-cut dress, perfect for dancing. She'd convinced herself the dark anthracite grey was sophisticated enough for a night out.

Because it had been her only choice.

When she'd looked for something to wear dancing, she'd found nothing suitable. Everything was too formal or conservative. Not frumpy, for she'd been taught to dress with elegance and care, but she had nothing *young* or *fun* in her wardrobe.

It was a sad statement about her life that at twenty-four she had nothing to wear for a night on the town.

Some night it had been.

Her fingers clenched and she pressed her knees together as she relived the heavy touch of grasping hands on her body, that hot breath on her face, the smell of wine and the slightly sour aftershave that had vied with the taste of panic on her tongue.

'Here.' It was Paul, holding out a steaming mug.

Eva blinked up, read his brooding expression and quickly focused on taking the drink without touching him.

That frown made her feel about six years old, caught in some misdemeanour.

Whereas she'd done nothing wrong.

She took a seat at the table, watched him take the seat opposite and raised her drink to her lips.

'Hot chocolate?' She'd thought he was making her coffee.

'Sugar's good for shock.' He paused. 'I'm assuming what happened was a shock?'

Eva slammed the mug down on the table as she swallowed the wrong way and began to choke. When the coughing finished, she glared at him.

'It was a complete surprise. He offered to take me to a taxi rank. I didn't expect or want...' She shook her head, her throat constricting.

'Then you shouldn't have headed into a deserted, dark alley with a stranger.' Paul's voice was brutally hard.

He was right. She'd been naïve, but the pounding

music, and sense of melancholy that had surrounded her since Paul had dropped his bombshell, had made her regret her decision to go to the club almost as soon as she'd arrived. Eva had been desperate to leave. She'd forced herself to stay for a couple of dances, as if needing to prove something to herself, though she didn't know what. When her dance partner had commiserated over her burgeoning headache and said he knew where there'd be a taxi waiting, it had seemed a good idea.

'It wasn't deserted. There were other people going out that way.'

'And that makes it okay?'

Once more Eva discovered the back of her eyes prickling with hot tears. She hated that Paul could make her feel so…so…

She shoved her chair back and shot to her feet.

Angry.

That was how he made her feel.

Angry at herself for being duped and for not taking better precautions. But angry with Paul, too, for continually needling her.

Eva refused to let him make her feel small. She'd already felt that way tonight. Small, weak, vulnerable and incredibly scared as she'd realised, in a moment's abrupt horror, how much she was at a stranger's mercy. How vast was the difference in physical power between them.

Despite the self-defence classes she'd so proudly taken, she'd felt at a loss. As if she couldn't believe this was happening to *her*.

A lifetime's training in good manners had had her asking more than once that he let her go, instead of taking action instantly. Her brain had taken for ever to catch up with the fact she was being groped against her will and needed to *do* something. Even when she'd kneed him it had only stopped him temporarily and she'd been too frozen to the spot to escape back into the club, watching in horror as he regrouped.

All this shot through her mind in a flash, while her anger bubbled from simmering to boiling point.

'I don't appreciate your attitude, Paul.'

There was no need for him to grind her down into the dirt with his disapproval. She already felt as if she'd been dragged through it tonight.

'*My* attitude?' He rocketed to his feet, palms planted on the table. 'I'm the one who saved you, remember?'

His words cut through her indignation. What would have happened if he hadn't been there?

Eva stared down at the red marks on one of his hands, a graze, a reminder that he'd put himself between her and her attacker. Her stomach churned.

'Thank you.' The words came out stiffly, her vocal cords constricted and her chest tight as a drum, making it hard to catch her breath. 'I don't remember if I thanked you before. I appreciate what you did.'

She surveyed him for signs of injury but saw none. He'd wiped off the mark she'd seen on his face before she could determine what it was.

Paul shrugged then lowered those wide shoulders a fraction. 'You're welcome.'

Yet the silence that followed bristled.

Eva swallowed again but it was no good. The words on her tongue insisted on spilling out.

'What, exactly, is your problem? You're not...' She waved one hand in a vague gesture. 'You're different.'

'*I'm* different? What about you? Haring off like that and—'

Her hackles rose again. 'I wasn't aware I had to get your permission before leaving the palace.'

Tonight her world had shattered. Her hopes and plans as well as her heart. Was it surprising she hadn't meekly toddled off to bed?

'Now you're being ridiculous. You know it wasn't a matter of permission.' He shoved his hands deep into his trouser pockets, the movement emphasising the breadth of his chest and the solidity of his thighs. His clenched jaw was the epitome of angry masculinity.

Her body responded eagerly to all that raw virility. The quickening in her blood and a clenching between her thighs felt like the ultimate betrayal.

Ridiculous, was she?

Her nostrils flared and she gathered herself up to her full height. 'If it's not about permission then what?'

'You're my fiancée, Eva. Don't you think I care for your well being?'

She blinked, stunned by his blind disregard for the truth.

Heat thrummed through her, indignation rising at his selective memory. For seconds she grappled with the dictates that had become second nature after a lifetime of royal obedience. To behave graciously. To smooth over ruffled feelings and restore harmony.

But she couldn't do it. Not tonight. Not after what had happened. She couldn't obediently agree and pretend she'd done something wrong. She'd spent four years holding back, pretending and hiding her feelings. That stopped now.

Eva took a step towards him, hands fisted at her sides, her shoulders back and her spine straight. Coolly, with all the hauteur seven centuries of royal breeding could conjure, she lifted her chin.

'First, I'm not your fiancée, Paul. You're dumping me, remember?'

Scowling, he opened his mouth to reply, but she was too quick, speaking as she closed the distance between them. 'Second, even if I were your fiancée, I have a right to go out to a public venue if I want.'

'I'm not disputing that, Eva—'

'In fact, if I'd chosen to visit every night club and bar in the city, that would still have been my choice, not yours.'

She swallowed, her throat scratchy. 'I admit I made a mistake. Following Fabrice outside wasn't a wise decision, though I thought, given the fact there were others around, it would be safe.'

'That's just where—'

'*But*,' she forged on, unwilling to allow argument, 'what I really can't stand is the fact that you blame *me* for being attacked. As if I should have *known* what he intended. As if I didn't have a right to feel safe in your capital. As if...' she paused and dragged air into lungs that had stopped working '...finding fault with the victim is easier than blaming a man who thinks he has a right to assault a woman just because he fancies her.'

Paul's scowl had vanished and his piercing blue eyes were wide with what looked like shock.

'I've got news for you, Paul.' Her finger jabbed his sternum, his chest just as immoveable as it looked. 'It's attitudes like yours that make this world unsafe for innocent women and girls. As if men can't be responsible for their actions around them. I'd thought better of you. I never thought you'd resort to victim-shaming.'

Her vocal cords closed around her last words but Eva stood firm, her eyes locked on his.

Hell and damnation!

Paul raked his hand back through his hair as he met Eva's fierce stare. Her eyes blazed with seething, silvery fire that made her look like a disdainful goddess.

He went to speak then shook his head. She was right. Her scorn burned him all over.

His mouth dried as he went back through their conversations. No wonder she'd thought he was blaming her, when all the time the real target of his ferocity was the man in the alley. And himself.

Paul should have done a better job of protecting her. He knew their earlier, abortive conversation had some part to play in her decision to go off alone tonight. But he'd taken his anger and frustration out on her.

Dragging his hands from his pockets, he spread them wide. 'I'm sorry, Eva. You're right. I made it sound like this is all your fault. I apologise.

That militant sparkle still flashed in her gaze but she drew a deep breath, as if relaxing a little.

A tiny part of him wondered what had happened to the woman whose thoughts and emotions he couldn't read. That Eva had disappeared completely.

But mainly he was consumed with shame. The last thing she needed was someone berating her after what had happened.

'I got a fright and lashed out. It's no excuse, I know.'

'*You* got a fright?' She sounded disbelieving.

Her jabbing finger dropped from his chest and, weirdly, he missed the connection. The feel of her touching him. Because the contact had been reassuring. He still couldn't banish the thought of what might have happened to her if he hadn't arrived when he had.

Nausea twisted his gut and the skin across his neck and shoulders prickled as it drew tight. He'd heard what her attacker had promised in retribution for her defensive knee to the groin. He only hoped that, since he'd spoken Ancillan, and coarse slang at that, Eva hadn't understood.

Paul's blood had run cold at the threat to her.

He couldn't recall ever feeling as furious as he had tonight. Even facing the full extent of his father's appalling legacy. Then he'd been angry, but it had been nothing like the red mist that had filled his vision as that loser had pawed Eva.

Something had snapped. He'd wanted to break her attacker's hands.

'I was petrified,' he admitted. 'At what might have happened if I hadn't reached you in time.'

Her eyes widened and the martial light left her gaze.

'It would have been nasty,' she admitted slowly. 'But I'd have screamed, and there were others nearby. Someone would have helped.'

Paul said nothing. He couldn't be so sanguine about her chances. But saying so might amplify any fear she felt after tonight's events.

'What?' Her brow puckered, as if she read his churning thoughts.

He shook his head. 'I still feel guilty. I should have protected you better.'

Logic decreed that was impossible, since she'd abandoned his protection to go clubbing alone, yet it was true. Eva and he were connected.

Her chin jerked up. 'I'm not your responsibility any more, remember?'

It amazed him that she'd ever fooled the world, and him in particular, that she was cool to the point of remoteness. He could almost hear the crack and sizzle of her temper.

It was…invigorating.

'I can't help it, Eva. Like it or not, there's a link between us.'

He waited for her to berate him but instead her mouth crimped in a way he'd never seen before. Her chin crumpled and when she lifted her hand to brush her long hair back off her shoulder he saw it shake.

'Eva?' He stepped nearer, so they stood toe to toe. A faint waft of scent teased him, something light and floral. Inviting.

He captured her wrist. Her pulse raced and fine tremors vibrated under his touch. His concern notched up. Maybe her attacker had hurt her worse than Paul had thought. Or perhaps she was coming down from the adrenaline overload as shock set in.

'What can I do?' He bent his head, trying to catch her eye, but she'd dropped her gaze to somewhere near his chin.

She dragged in a shuddery breath. 'Don't be nice to me.'

He frowned, trying to fathom what was going on. 'You'd rather I was angry with you?'

This time her lips curved in a wobbly approximation of a smile that made pain pierce his chest. She was hurting, and he discovered he hated that.

She shook her head and he watched, fascinated, as her long hair slipped over her shoulders. Earlier, in the gloom, he'd thought it seductive. Now it threatened to distract him totally. He wanted to reach out and...

'Come and sit down. Drink your hot chocolate. You'll feel better.'

She lifted her chin and met his eyes, just for a moment. He couldn't read her expression now. It reminded him of when they'd been together at the palace, talking about ending their betrothal.

She looked away. 'Thanks, but I don't want hot chocolate.'

Paul curved his other hand round her upper arm, her skin like cool silk.

'You're shaking.'

She shrugged. 'It will pass.'

Not good enough. Paul was used to taking action. Making things happen. Fixing problems.

'There must be something I can do. Something that would help.'

Another half-smile, this time unmistakeably wry.

'What?'

'It's nothing.'

Paul frowned. If there was one thing he'd learned tonight, it was that Eva could be forthright when she wanted to be. Why wasn't she now?

Releasing her wrist, he curled his finger under her chin, lifting it so he could hold her gaze.

His breath stalled as he saw how forlorn she looked.

His other hand stroked up her arm to her bare shoulder and back down to grasp her hand.

'It will be all right, Eva. Truly. It's over now.'

Her tiny huff of amusement was unexpected. 'Yes. You're right. It's over.'

But, though her posture was as perfect as ever and her stare direct, he wasn't fooled. It wasn't just the fact that she still trembled. It was the expression in her eyes.

'Eva. Tell me what I can do to help.'

For a long moment he thought she wasn't going to say anything. Then he heard, 'Kiss me. I want you to kiss me.'

CHAPTER FIVE

PAUL STARED AT her as if no woman had ever wanted to kiss him before. His eyebrows lifted from their deep V of concern and his eyes widened.

At least he looked stunned rather than sorry for her. That was an improvement.

When he'd been kind, Eva's heart had twisted. She'd had a tough night in so many ways and sympathy would only crack her veneer of calm. She'd feared she might slip up and reveal her feelings for him.

And when he'd said there was a link between them…
She hadn't known whether to laugh or cry.

She'd been the one to recognise that link years ago. To treasure it and dream of a future built on it. Paul had been completely oblivious.

If he'd felt that link tonight…

No, it was just that he felt some responsibility since, in the eyes of the world, they were to be married.

'Eva? What are you saying?'

Her lips firmed as she fought despair with anger.

'You heard me, Paul.'

She wasn't going to say it again. Even though it was true. The one thing that at this moment would make her feel better was Paul's lips on hers, blotting out tonight's bitter regrets and searing hurt. Giving her the solace of his caress.

His frown was back, deeper than ever. His hand beneath her chin moved to her shoulder. To hold her at a distance or to deliver a paternal pat of solace? As if she didn't know her own mind.

He'd asked what she wanted and she'd told him.

Abruptly, gloriously, she didn't care what he thought. Only that this was the last chance she'd ever have to kiss the man she'd adored since she'd been fifteen. The man who'd cracked her heart wide open and didn't even know it.

Tomorrow—later this morning—she'd say goodbye to him for ever. For now, they were alone, and she still wanted so much more than he'd ever give her.

Instinct told her to grab this opportunity for just a moment's solace, and that was what she did. One hand settled on that hard, straight shoulder. The other curled around the back of his neck, learning the texture of hot skin and soft hair. She rose on her toes and pulled his head down.

Paul stared down into the face of a woman he didn't know. Felt her hands on him, surprisingly strong, and stopping her didn't enter his brain.

Curiosity buzzed, stronger than surprise.

And something more than curiosity. Something that made his heart leap in his chest as soft lips settled against his.

That mouth. How had he not recognised that mouth for what it was? Pure seduction.

Her lips brushed his, making his breath still and his grip on her waist tighten.

He couldn't even recall reaching for Eva. But now he couldn't imagine relinquishing his hold. Her waist was narrow but he felt the sensual curve that led to the flare of her hips. Even the slippery satin of her dress—the dress that had taunted him from the moment he'd seen her in it—felt like an invitation.

She was so alluringly feminine. Delicious curves. Decadently inviting lips. A body that stretched seductively up against his, her breasts cushioning him in a way that bent his self-control out of shape.

From the first touch of her hand at his neck he'd gone rigid. The caress of her lips on his sent bolts of searing tension straight to his groin.

Once more she kissed him, a light caress that hinted at passion but was more tease than anything. Then, as his fingers tightened around her middle, she gasped and finally her tongue flicked out to trace his lips.

Instantly Paul took the lead. Because tantalising caresses simply weren't enough. She'd woken the need he'd kept stringently under control for four long years. That, and his curiosity to know this new, unexpected Eva, dragged him straight into temptation.

Once he tasted her, there was no going back.

Sweet and distinctive like wild honey from the mountains. No other woman tasted like Eva. Then there was the tiny little humming sound that came from the back of her throat and sounded like approval and invitation.

He opened his mouth and sucked in her tongue.

Paul felt her jolt of surprise, wondered at it then forgot

about it as he concentrated on the sensations of her tongue in his mouth and the quiver of her body against him.

His hands were possessive. He wanted to haul her close, but he had enough control not to. Not after her experience tonight.

Yet she *was* flush against him, not because he'd dragged her there but because she'd closed the space between them.

His eyes closed at the sinuous movement of her soft body against his, igniting molten fire in his groin. He tried to ignore it, but that left his brain free to concentrate on their kiss.

Eva's tongue curled around his then drew back. He followed, plunging into sweet heat, needing more. Was that a heartbeat's hesitation? No, he'd imagined it. If anything her hands clung tighter than before, fingers digging into him as she tilted her head and sucked him deeper with a desperation that matched his own.

He shuddered at the fierce wave of pleasure cresting within him. His hands tightened at her waist and his body canted forward, bending her back, striving to absorb the flavour of her, the piercingly arousing perfection of Eva in his arms offering so much.

Eva, the woman he'd thought he'd known.

He'd known nothing.

Tonight was a revelation. Not just of her but of his own feelings. He'd imagined what he felt for her was simply duty. But when put to the test he discovered nothing about his relationship with Eva was what it seemed. *She* wasn't what she seemed.

She only had to pout those pretty lips and flash those bright eyes and he wanted everything.

Paul's guard slipped completely when he heard it again, and felt it too—that humming vibration of approval that came from Eva's mouth and trembled across his tongue. It was a lover's invitation.

How was he supposed to resist? That tiny sound alone was enough to test even a man trained in self-denial from years of celibacy.

Her thighs shifted restlessly against his, her body tantalising as she moved, cushioning his hardening erection against her belly.

The force of his arousal stunned him. It was so instantaneous, so complete. So unbelievable after years of implacable control. In the past he'd ground down any inclination for sex with long hours of work, achieving the impossible, because it was his duty to save his nation and he refused to countenance failure.

But now, with Eva supple and seductive in his arms, he couldn't focus on duty. Even the simple dictates of his conscience, telling him not to take advantage of a woman who was suffering from shock, seemed beyond him.

Her hands palmed his cheeks then his shoulders to settle splayed on his chest, where his heart hammered. He felt her touch like a brand, a scorching incentive to take more.

Finally, with a last burst of determination, he lifted his head. But the action was a hollow victory because he ached for her with every cell of his being. He didn't want to do the right thing. He wanted to kiss Eva. He wanted to delight in her eager body and passionate kisses and...

'Don't stop!'

Paul gritted his teeth and closed his eyes, blotting out the beguiling sight of her wide eyes, now more blue than grey, beseeching him.

As if she wanted exactly what he wanted.

What he couldn't allow himself to take.

'Eva.' His voice was unrecognisable, a strained rumble, as if it came from some distant chasm far below the earth's surface. He tried again, opening his eyes to meet her gaze, ignoring the jolt of response that hit him like an unseen blow as their gazes locked. 'Eva, we can't do this. You're not thinking—'

'Don't you *dare* try to tell me I don't know what I want!'

Anger made her eyes glitter but, instead of withdrawing, she stayed pressed against him.

She'd never looked so magnificent.

Inevitably his admiration made itself known in the most obvious way. An expression he couldn't identify crossed her features as his erection stirred against her.

'I wouldn't dream of it.' Especially when he didn't want to stop either. Yet Paul couldn't shake the conviction that he needed to protect her, even from himself. 'But you've had a shock and it would be wrong to take advantage of that. You're not yourself.'

Her nostrils flared and her mouth turned down in the corners in a way that should have made her look unattractive but instead turned into the sexiest, sultriest pout he'd ever seen.

The throb of need that pulsed through his body almost undid him.

'Because you don't really want me. You just feel sorry for me.'

Paul couldn't contain the crack of laugher that escaped his lips. 'You know I want you. I can't disguise that.'

How much more obvious could it be, with his erection hard against her and his control hanging by a thread? He didn't yet have the power to pull away.

On that thought, he finally managed to do what he should have done earlier. He stepped back, coming up against the huge kitchen table that filled the centre of the room.

Eva moved a split second later, following him. Her luscious body blanketed his, fraying his tattered determination. He was trying to do the decent thing but she made it tough.

'Eva...' Her name turned into a sigh as she grabbed one of his hands and put it to her breast. Convulsively his fingers closed on satin and warm, rounded flesh. Her eyes darkened as he squeezed. Her gaze turned the hazy blue of the sea at dawn.

She was killing him.

Then his eyes rolled back in his head as she cupped his erection with her other hand. His breath hissed and his body turned to stone. All except that throbbing, eager part of him that surged harder against her touch.

'Kiss me, Paul. Please.'

Her lips were against his, inviting him. The perfect swell of her breast was in his hand and the possessive clasp of her fingers around him obliterated all thought.

Paul kissed her. Hard.

It wasn't enough. He wanted all her sweetness. He wanted...

Dazed, he let himself savour the heady prospect of

her giving him exactly what he wanted—relief from the tangle of frustrated longing, thwarted passion and the inhibiting voice of his conscience that told him to move away.

This was just a moment's fantasy, not reality.

Yet he exhaled with relief and something close to despair as Eva tugged his zip down and slid her fingers inside his trousers to hold him, her soft hand against hard, needy flesh.

Lightning seared his blackened vision, strobe lights of white-hot energy that arced and whirled as Eva tested his length, then squeezed.

Air expelled from his lungs in a guttural rush. There was a thrumming in his ears as he tried to collect his scattered control.

He'd be strong again in a second. When he had time to regroup. Except now, somehow, he held both her breasts in his hands, testing their weight, revelling in the graze of her pebbled nipples. Barely, he resisted the need to strip away the flimsy satin dress so he could feast on her ripeness.

Then she was undoing his belt with her other hand.

It was exactly what he wanted and everything he shouldn't.

He opened his mouth to stop her when Eva's mouth collided with his again. The movement was clumsy, almost desperate, but so beautiful that he felt himself sink back into the bliss of the moment.

Paul's whole body trembled. He relinquished her breasts, wrapping one arm round her and using the other to push back her long hair that had fallen forward, caressing his cheek.

It was incredibly soft, impossibly decadent, that long skein of silk that somehow wrapped itself around his fingers, just as she wrapped her fingers around him, stroking, teasing.

He had to let her go. Make her release him too.

But then, before he could act, there it was, thundering towards him like a freight train racing down a mountain. Paul felt the building pressure, the torture of a body grown too taut and hard to contain itself. The careering rush of pleasure.

He just had enough time to read Eva's wide-eyed look of elation, and cover the head of his erection with his hand, before he convulsed, helpless, against the sudden, raw rush of ecstasy.

Eva was stunned.

How could a man be magnificently powerful and at the same time so vulnerable?

The sight of Paul lost in the throes of climax, the feel of him jerkily pulsing in her hand, was the most exciting thing she'd known.

Watching his big shoulders judder, seeing him fling his head back, the tendons in his throat standing proud, made him seem not weak but incredibly strong.

Despite the fact he was at her mercy.

The knowledge floored her.

No, this wasn't about knowledge, it was about the visceral feeling, the love, compassion and deep sense of connection.

How she loved the feel of him, satin-soft yet impossibly hard, beneath her hand. The feel of him shuddering with pleasure at her touch.

Hers. Not someone else's but hers. *She'd* done that. Brought sexual fulfilment to the man she loved.

Pinpricks of delight exploded through her.

Even when he bowed his head and nudged her hand aside, those great, racking shudders easing to small tremors, she was dumbstruck by the power she'd unleashed.

She'd had no idea it could be like this. So intense, so exciting. Because of course theory was no substitute for reality. Her knowledge of sex, apart from a few pretty innocent kisses, was all theoretical.

Even the heavy musk scent in the air and the sound of Paul's laboured breaths were something completely new.

New and exhilarating. Though she still felt that edgy, needy sensation between her thighs, making her shift her weight to ease it.

She sighed, trying to ignore her own needs. Instead she took in the dull flush of colour across Paul's high cheek bones, the heavy-lidded look from glittering eyes that spoke of sensuality and satisfaction.

A shiver ripped through her and headed straight to her sex. Everything inside her softened.

Watching Paul come, *feeling* his potent explosion, was the single most exciting moment of her life.

He turned away, cleaning himself up, and Eva supposed she should do the same. Her hand was sticky. But she stayed where she was, her brain whirring on overdrive, her body revved. Because she loved how she'd affected him.

Just for a short time, he'd been *hers*.

Their kiss had been everything she'd hoped for. Passionate, beautiful and definitely mutual. Her heart had soared. Yet she'd feared it wouldn't last. She'd known Paul would pull away, because she was the fiancée he no longer wanted. And she'd been right, though he'd couched his rejection in terms of looking after her, not wanting to take advantage.

Take advantage! Was that what *she'd* done? Shoving her hand in his trousers?

Even now she could barely believe she'd done that. It was so out of character.

Because all her life she'd conformed, agreed, been polite and never pushed for what she wanted. Except when her parents had asked if she wanted to marry Paul of St Ancilla and she'd said yes.

But all those years of polite waiting, of doing the right thing, being gracious and amenable, hadn't got her what she wanted. Because Paul had never wanted her, Eva. Just a royal princess who'd do her royal duty and, as a bonus, bring her fortune with her.

Something had snapped in her tonight. Maybe because of the danger she'd been in at the hands of a stranger. Or maybe because Paul had snarked at her, as if she'd been to blame.

Whatever the cause, Eva had finally had enough. She was about to lose him. That knowledge had spurred her on to kiss him, touch him, as she'd previously only dreamed of. To snatch at least a moment for herself.

It had been glorious.

But now it was over.

She heard the sound of his zip, saw the straight set of his shoulders as he turned on a tap, his back still to her. Paul hadn't looked at her once since that gleaming, sexually charged stare that had pierced straight to her womb.

Just thinking of it, another tremor raked her from head to toe. Once more it ended at that sensitive place between her legs.

Paul turned and she braced herself for rejection.

His face was unreadable, his features tight, the curve of his cheek and the angle of his jaw pronounced. He looked more handsome than ever and even more un-attainable.

Eva's heart dropped.

His mouth twisted up in a grimace that reinforced her fears. 'I'm sorry, Eva.'

'Sorry?' she parroted. She should be the one apologising. She'd been the one to force him to kiss her, to touch him.

He closed the space between them with a couple of strides and she found herself pressed up against the table.

'I lost control.' His brow furrowed into a scowl.

'I know.' And it had been glorious, but she didn't say that. 'You didn't…enjoy it?'

Now she was confused. Surely that powerful climax told its own story?

The scowl eased a little and the curl of his lip looked a fraction softer. 'Of course I enjoyed it. But I shouldn't have. I don't know what came over me. One touch.' His voice lowered to a mutter. 'One touch and I was done for.' He shook his head. 'I showed all the finesse and self-control of a teenager.'

Eva tilted her head, trying to gauge whether it was embarrassment or genuine regret behind his words.

'What's the problem? That you came so fast or that it was me that made you?'

Her eyes widened a little as the words shot from her mouth, for this was the sort of straight talking she never engaged in. She raised her chin too. She wasn't ashamed of what she'd done.

Unless Paul saw it as some sort of assault. The idea made her flesh crawl. Had she been so wrapped up in her own desire she'd misunderstood his protests? How unwilling had he been?

His crooked smile eased her fears. 'I'm a big boy, Eva. If I hadn't wanted your touch, I'd have fended you off.'

So he'd *wanted* her touch.

The constriction that had hampered her last few breaths eased.

'I'm not usually so gauche.' Another shake of his head. 'But it's been a long time since a woman touched me.'

'It has?' She'd imagined that with his looks and charm he'd have a bevy of women waiting to provide comfort to the lonely Prince who saw so little of his fiancée.

Paul's gaze caught hers. 'Of course. We've been engaged for four years. I exchanged promises with you and I take my word seriously.'

Eva had thought by now she'd withstood every shock the night could possibly have in store. She was wrong. She stared up at him, eyes bulging.

'You mean...?' She shook her head, then paused to shove her hair back from her face when it obscured her vision. 'You've been celibate all this time?'

It seemed impossible. Paul abstaining from sexual pleasure because of her.

'I made a promise to be loyal to you as my bride-to-be. I don't break my promises.'

Eva couldn't tell if that was pride, hauteur or disapproval stiffening his tall form.

'I take it you didn't feel the same?' His tone was austere. 'I suppose you wouldn't. We're only together a couple of times a year.'

'That wasn't my choice.' Her hands slid to her hips. 'I offered to visit more often but you said no.' That still rankled. During the first year of their engagement, she'd only seen him twice!

'Only because I've been very busy. I didn't have time to entertain you on a social visit.'

Eva drew a deep breath and counted to ten. 'Maybe I don't need entertaining. Maybe I wanted to support you.'

It was clear from Paul's stunned stare that the thought had never occurred to him. Which was typical of their non-relationship, wasn't it?

Suddenly Eva was tired of all this. The false relationship, the tiptoeing around the truth. It was over and that was that.

Even her breaking heart and the ache of rejection could wait till tomorrow. For now, she just wanted to escape. There was no reason to stay for a post mortem on their engagement. Or to rehash tonight's events.

She turned towards the door, already forming words of farewell. Except long fingers wrapped around her arm, stopping her.

Immediate heat flashed through her. Excitement. Need.

Eva hated that she couldn't prevent her reaction to him. But it was time to face facts. Whatever they'd shared was over.

Yet when she tried to free her arm Paul captured her other arm too, his long fingers gentle but implacable.

'Where do you think you're going?' His voice dropped an octave, rumbling across her skin on an unfamiliar note that made her insides clench.

Eva looked up but didn't meet those keen eyes. 'Tonight has been a disaster. It's time we went our separate ways, don't you think?'

'You've got to be kidding. We've barely started.'

Stunned as much by Paul's unmistakably suggestive tone as by his words, she met his gaze. And couldn't look away. His expression made her hot inside. Hotter than she already was.

He released one arm and lifted his hand to her face, long fingers sliding gently across her cheek to her mouth, his thumb capturing her bottom lip and pressing till she opened for him. Instantly, without her consciously planning it, her tongue slipped out to lick him, drawing the taste of him—hot, salty male—into her mouth.

Those dark blue eyes flared and his mouth rucked up in an approving smile.

'No, I don't believe we're anywhere near finished.'

For the second time in one night she looked into the face of a man with sex on his mind. But this wasn't a stranger who dismayed or disgusted her. The roaring rush of blood in her ears and the catapulting thump of her heart were all about excitement.

Paul's head lowered, slowly enough that she could

turn away if she wanted. Instead Eva tilted her chin higher, meeting his lips with hers.

Eva was struck by how familiar it felt. The shape of Paul's mouth on hers, the taste and scent of him, something fresh like pine trees and the outdoors. The wonderful warmth of his body against hers, his embrace enfolding her.

It didn't even matter that this was simply sex, not love. If this was all she'd have of Paul before they parted, she'd take it gladly.

She slid her hands up his broad chest to link around the back of his neck, the ends of her fingers tunnelling through his hair. Surprising how intimate that felt, given how she'd touched him earlier.

A chuckle bubbled inside her, but died when powerful hands palmed her buttocks and lifted her off the floor. Her eyes snapped open and for a moment she lost herself in his indigo gaze.

He moved and then she was sitting on the table with Paul standing wedged between her thighs.

Heat squirmed through her, making her shift on the scrubbed surface.

'What…?'

But then he was kissing her again, tenderly, thoroughly, learning her and what she liked. It seemed she liked everything, from the gentle bite of his teeth on her bottom lip that made her nipples tingle, to the languorously slow kisses that made her melt inside.

Her eyelids were heavy and her body fluid with pleasure when she registered his hands on her legs. Their kiss didn't falter as her hem crept up her thighs and his hand slid down to cup wet silk.

Eva moaned into his mouth, her hips tilting needily.

Another caress, another circle of her hips, and the hunger for fulfilment grew. Was this how Paul had felt when she'd caressed him, at first tentatively, then with determination?

There was nothing tentative about Paul's touch. He knew exactly what he was doing. Looping an arm around her waist, he lifted her off the table just enough to drag her silk underwear down. Then he backed away from her, rolling her panties down her bare legs.

And still their lips were locked, his tongue stroking hers, then delving rhythmically into her mouth in a way that made her even more restless.

Finally, he touched her again between the legs. A slow, sliding caress through damp folds that nearly had her jumping off the table.

Eva moaned against his mouth then stopped as he pulled away. Appalled, she met his knowing gaze. Was he going to stop? He couldn't, surely? Not when he made her feel…

'Patience, Eva.' He lifted her hand to his mouth, but instead of a courtly kiss to the back of her hand he held her gaze and licked her from the inside of her wrist, across her palm and right to the end of her fingers, drawing them into his mouth and sucking.

A dart of fire shot from her nipples to her womb, exploding in shuddering waves. Her internal muscles clenched and her breath hissed in sharply.

Looking into that proud, determined face, Eva realised she didn't know Paul as well as she'd imagined. This flagrant carnality was a side of him she'd never suspected when she'd imagined his kisses and, yes, sex.

She'd known being with him would be wonderful because she loved him. But the earthy appreciation in his expression as he looked down her body to where his fingers teased was something she hadn't expected.

Eva felt she should be shocked. Instead she was incredibly aroused.

And he knew. It was there in the triumphant look he gave her from under those straight black eyebrows.

She opened her mouth to say something but words eluded her. Then he was gone, sinking to his knees before her. One hard yank dragged her right to the edge of the table and then, while she watched in disbelief, he leaned in to kiss her.

It was like watching a film in slow motion. Each frame froze as she struggled to take in what she was seeing. Then, with the touch of his mouth on her most sensitive skin, the film sped up to match her racketing pulse.

Eva stared, trying to connect the sight of Paul between her legs and the exquisitely arousing sensations as he used his tongue and lips to pleasure her.

It didn't take much. She was ready for him, so on edge. What he made her feel was wondrous, so exactly what she needed, that soon she teetered on the brink of losing herself.

It was the sight of Paul looking up that did it. The expression of satisfaction in his gaze as it met hers, as if the pair of them shared a delicious secret, that sent her over the edge.

Fingers clamped on the table, legs spread wide by his shoulders, Eva tossed her head back and screamed as ecstasy took her.

It went on and on, writhing through her, a pleasure so intense it came close to pain, except that this made her feel as if she'd shot to heaven.

Eyes closed, all she could do was cling on and ride out the waves of powerful sensation. Till somehow it wasn't wood that she clutched but Paul, his shoulders hard beneath her clenching fingers, his arms tight around her, his voice rough but reassuring in her ear.

Foggily, Eva wondered if it was possible she'd died and gone to paradise. Then she gave up trying to think and slumped into his strong arms.

CHAPTER SIX

Eva fitted his hold perfectly. Strange that he hadn't considered that before. Even when they'd danced at various
balls he hadn't realised how good she'd feel against him.

He'd been aware of her femininity, of course. You
couldn't waltz with a woman like Eva and not be drawn
to her. But in the past he'd been busy trying to find a
way through her reserve, frustrated at her aloofness.
Sometimes, when her conversation had consisted of
platitudes and she'd barely met his eyes, he'd focused
his mind instead on the most pressing of the nation's
debts and his plans to reduce them.

Now she had his full attention.

She'd had it since she'd swept into the ball, head
high and with a light in her eyes he'd never seen before.

There was so much about Eva he'd never seen or
suspected before.

Her fiery anger.

Her obstinacy.

Her passion.

Her ability to take him from zero to a blistering climax in what felt like seconds.

His belly clenched and heat eddied deep inside. Paul

was torn between shame at how he'd come apart so easily and the burning need to have her touch him again.

As for the sight of her losing herself with such abandon, the scent and wild honey taste of her...

He hefted her higher in his arms and strode from the kitchen towards the tower's spiral staircase. He knew every step of the way but was glad of the low-level sensor lighting that sprang up on the steps. He didn't want to stumble with Eva in his embrace.

She turned her face into his neck, but gave no other sign of being awake.

Paul smiled. Her orgasm had left her soft as a sleepy kitten against him. It made a change from the defiant, obstinate woman who'd made her appearance tonight. And from the coolly distant fiancée who'd visited St Ancilla for years.

He was determined to discover which of them was the real Eva.

As he strode higher he quickly reviewed practicalities. They needed time alone and here at the lodge they'd have privacy, more so than at the palace.

Key staff knew where he was. The car had a tracker and he'd used handprint security to enter the house, at the same time remotely locking the gates. Staff could contact him in an emergency. No doubt there was a guard on duty now in the discreet security building near the front gate.

But, with any luck, no one would need him for the next twenty-four hours. He'd kept a full day free of appointments, knowing that his plans to end the engagement would mean he'd need to be available to discuss the details with Eva. To agree on how and when they'd announce the news of their separation.

Now, with her hair tickling his chin, her delicious body in his embrace and the scent of sex and spring flowers tantalising his nostrils, the end of their betrothal was the last thing on his mind.

For years Paul had stifled his libido as best he could, working to the point of exhaustion. He hadn't fully succeeded but he hadn't given in to its urges.

Tonight he had. Spectacularly.

And the most intriguing thing was that, despite his clumsiness, his ego-bruising gaucheness at coming the way he had, the last half-hour with Eva had rivalled any sex he could recall.

He reached the top of the stairs and shouldered his way into the suite he kept for himself, a round room with windows on three sides and an *en suite* bathroom. No lights were on here, but the curtains at one window were open and he had no trouble finding his way.

Moments later he lowered Eva onto the bed. She stretched, turning her head into the pillow and arching her back. It was an instinctive, sensual movement and it dragged the tension in his belly up another notch.

He liked having Eva in his bed, her hair spilling like a dark cloud around her pale shoulders. Her legs bare and her toes curling.

Paul recalled the thud as her high heels had dropped unheeded to the kitchen floor as she screamed her release, and the skin across his neck and shoulders prickled.

Reaching back, he grabbed his lightweight sweater at the neck and hauled it over his head, tossing it onto a nearby chair. He looked forward to having Eva in his arms again, skin to skin.

The thought sent a luxurious shiver through him as he bent to rifle the bedside table, hoping to find... Yes, he was in luck. There at the back of the drawer was a box of condoms. He opened it, dropping its contents onto the top of the table.

'What are you doing?' There it was again, that husky note he'd heard in Eva's voice for the first time tonight. It rasped across the tight skin of his belly, sending another surge of heat to his groin.

She lay on her side and had raised herself on one elbow. Even in the gloom he appreciated the feminine allure of her silhouette, the deepened dip to her waist and the sweet curve up to her hips.

Paul's throat dried. 'Making sure we have protection.'

In this light he didn't see her move but he'd swear she stiffened.

'Aren't you taking a lot for granted?'

But, when her gaze turned from the table to him, he heard her indrawn breath as she surveyed his bare torso.

Paul wasn't vain but he knew his wide-shouldered frame, kept trim by his love of sport, drew female attention. Now, as he felt Eva's gaze track from his ribs to his belt, he bit back a smile.

He sat beside her, one hand planted on the bed beyond her hip.

'What, you were going to take your pleasure from me then just walk away?'

She shifted, wriggling up the bed towards the pillows. In the process he felt the brush of her legs and inhaled again the heady scent of warm woman and sex. His trousers tightened against his groin but he didn't move.

'You've already…taken *your* pleasure.'

Was that embarrassment he heard? Surely not from the woman who'd thrust her hand into his pants!

He shuddered at the memory of her soft palm sliding along his length, her fingers encircling him. She'd been a little clumsy but that had only added to the piquancy, proof that she was too eager for finesse.

Paul laughed, the sound rusty with barely suppressed desire. 'That was just a start, Eva.' He had plans for the rest of the night and they didn't include sleep. 'When a man's fiancée shows she's eager for sex—'

'I'm not your fiancée.'

Paul refused to touch that one. He had more pressing things on his mind than another argument.

He lifted his hand to trail his fingers down her satin-clad thigh. 'But you want me, don't you, lover?'

Her breath hissed in and he felt her tremble. Yet he made himself stop, his fingertips barely touching the place where satin met smooth, enticing flesh. It was surprising how difficult it was not to caress her. Once he'd touched her and tasted her, he wanted so much more.

'You want to have sex?'

Once more he found her tone difficult to read. That almost sounded like doubt in her voice. As if he'd left any doubts about his desire for her!

'Absolutely.' He swallowed hard. 'I suspect we'll be phenomenal together.'

When still she said nothing, Paul frowned and made himself lift his hand away.

After what they'd done downstairs it seemed impossible but perhaps, after all, he'd read Eva wrong and she didn't want…

A slim hand grabbed his and settled it palm-down on her bare thigh.

Paul's heart leapt high in his throat, the throb in his groin pulsing even harder.

He splayed his fingers, sliding them round her silky skin, and she shifted, parting her legs a little to give him better access.

Doubt vanished in a flash, replaced by excitement.

Eva's heartbeat quickened as Paul caressed her leg in long, deliberate strokes. They were as easy and regular as waves rippling in to shore, but with each slide of his hand her pulse pounded harder and she became more aware of that aching spot between her thighs.

He reached down to circle her ankles and calves, pausing to massage her soles, and a blissful sigh escaped. She tried to tell herself it was because she'd worn high heels for hours but even a woman as innocent as she knew the difference between relaxation and arousal.

By the time Paul worked his way back up her other leg to the hem of her dress, she was twitching and eager for so much more.

'I want to see all of you, Eva.' His low voice burred across her skin as he pushed the material up her thighs in slow, breath-stealing increments.

It was what she wanted. Yet the thought of lying naked before him, like some carnal offering, made her supremely uneasy. She'd never been naked for any man. She wanted Paul, wanted to be possessed by him, but, despite what they'd just done to each other, shyness rose in a baffling wave.

How could she be shy after that scene in the kitchen?

Yet it was true. More, she feared revealing her inexperience. This was her only chance to make love with Paul. She was under no illusions that sex would alter his decision to call off their wedding. She'd take tonight gladly, though, and give him no reason to back off.

'You first.' Her tight vocal cords turned the words into a throaty command instead of a tentative suggestion.

Paul didn't seem to mind. He shrugged, those wide shoulders rising. She caught the white gleam of his smile. 'If you like.'

He half-turned from her and she clamped her mouth shut over an instinctive protest at the loss of contact. It took only seconds for him to remove his shoes and socks, then he was standing by the bed, shucking the rest of his clothes off, and Eva's eyes rounded at the sight of him.

Even in the half-light he was magnificent. Tall, lean but powerful across the chest, with a flat abdomen, narrow hips and long, muscled legs. His erection stood out proud and ready for her and Eva squeezed her thighs together as moist heat drenched her.

'Would you like to put the condom on me?' He picked up a packet from the table and tore it open.

Eva swallowed, torn between excitement and horror. She did want to, but if she fumbled too much he might guess she'd never done this before. It was a wonder he hadn't already. Down in the kitchen she'd acted on instinct rather than experience. Presumably he'd been too aroused to notice.

Four years of celibacy, he'd said. That must explain it. No wonder he'd been so responsive to her touch.

Her heart dipped. Paul's eager reaction hadn't been to *her* specifically. He'd been primed by abstinence to respond to a woman's caresses.

Even so, Eva wanted this. Wanted him. This was her one opportunity for intimacy with the man she still, despite everything, loved.

So much for pride. But pride was a cold bed-fellow. She craved the warmth of his loving, even if it was only a travesty of the emotional response she needed from him.

Whatever the reason, Paul wanted *her*. She couldn't refuse him or herself.

'No. I want to watch you do it.' Her voice was a rough croak but he didn't seem to mind.

Paul laughed. 'Do you, indeed? Well, it's probably better. I don't want to disgrace myself again like I did downstairs. This time I intend to last long enough to satisfy you.'

Eva's indrawn breath was fire and molten metal as her brain provided a picture of him doing just that.

Then he was on the bed, knees straddling her legs.

'Sit up, sweetheart.'

Eva's silly heart somersaulted at the casual endearment. Part of her brain screamed she was a fool. The other part urged her on.

She raised herself so Paul could reach behind to her zip. Slowly he peeled the narrow straps down her arms. Then gently, almost reverently, he undid her bra.

Any hesitation she felt about baring her breasts died as he leaned in and kissed her, murmuring how beautiful she was as he cupped her with his big, warm hands.

Heat shot through her, another arrowing dart of fire, and then she was on her back, lifting her hips as he dragged her dress down and away. Their knees bumped and she didn't know quite what to do with her hands. But none of that detracted from the shivery delight of Paul's hands on her, his mouth caressing hers, and that possessive-sounding growl as he palmed her bare hips.

Finally, they were naked. He turned her towards him so they lay on their sides, facing each other. Then he pulled back and looked down, grinning.

'You're exquisite.'

It was on the tip of her tongue to refute it, knowing he didn't mean it, but then his fingertips touched her nipple in the most delicate touch and her breath fractured.

When he touched her like that she *felt* different. Special. She imagined his eyes glowed with a light she hadn't seen before, even though common sense said she couldn't really read his expression. She tried to tell herself it was simply lust but her aching heart wanted to believe it was because at last Paul saw the woman she really was.

The harping voice of caution was silenced by the sheer magic of this moment with Paul.

His caresses as he skimmed her body brought fire in their wake, and when he bent to kiss her breast, then suck her nipple, Eva arched into him, a lightning bolt of desire ripping through her.

She was panting when finally, after exploring her

thoroughly with his hands and mouth, he rolled on top of her. Eva was bombarded with sensation. The weight of him, pressing her down onto the bed. He was taller and broader than her. It might have felt suffocating but instead she welcomed it, wrapping her arms around him. His skin was smooth as silk, swelling intriguingly over lean muscle and bone. His hairy legs tickled hers and the hair on his chest abraded her breasts so deliciously, her breath caught.

'You like that?' He settled more firmly between her legs, and that was new too, the feel of her thighs cradling his hot, hard body.

Eva nodded, her throat constricted. She didn't want to talk.

'What else do you like?' He propped himself on his elbows above her, his patient stillness as he waited for her response warring with the sexual promise implicit in his preternaturally still frame.

Eva didn't want to wait. She wanted him to deliver what his body promised.

'You, just you.'

She lifted her feet, hooking her ankles around the back of his thighs, feeling him sink deeper against her, his erection stiff and long. Almost daunting, but she refused to think that way. Instead Eva lifted her hands to the back of his head, driving her fingers through his thick hair, cupping his skull, pulling him down. 'I want you inside me. Now.'

Finally, he succumbed to her tugging and lowered his mouth to hers.

Once again she felt it. Not just the sharp tug of desire but the overwhelming tenderness of love. That it was all on her side no longer mattered. She wanted Paul so badly. He would be her first lover. That would be something wonderful, even though they were destined to go their separate ways tomorrow. At least she'd have the memory of tonight to take with her.

Paul's kiss was surprisingly tender. She felt a tremor of tension running through him and the heavy press of his erection. Eva sensed he was suppressing his own urgency for her benefit.

Then his hand slipped between them, his fingers arrowing straight to the achy, wet place between her thighs that throbbed with such need.

His head lifted and he smiled. A secret, intimate smile that tugged at her heart strings.

Then she had no time to think about anything but the extraordinary feeling of Paul pushing against her, into her, so full and heavy and…

Her breath fractured on a searing slash of pain. She stiffened all over at the sharp sting that went on and on. For some reason she hadn't expected it, assuming that years of riding and other exercise would have removed the physical proof of her virginity.

Paul froze. 'Eva?'

She watched his shoulders rise away from her as he pulled back.

Instantly she tightened the grip of her legs around him and grabbed at him, sinking her fingers in the taut flesh of his buttocks, pulling him close so that he sank deep inside.

Tears pricked the backs of her eyes at that final flash of pain, and she arched up. Eva rested her forehead against his hard collarbone, inhaling his reassuringly familiar, outdoorsy scent as she gasped for air.

The world stilled. She heard the thrum of her pulse in her ears and felt it pound through her whole body.

His hand stroked her head, making her long hair slide around her shoulders.

'Oh, Eva.' His deep voice was a caress in itself. 'It'll be all right soon.'

Finally, trembling, she sank back against the pillows. Above her she made out the wide line of Paul's shoulders against the darkness, and the glint of his eyes.

'Are you okay?'

Eva nodded. 'Fine.' She almost was. She just felt… disoriented, adjusting to the unaccustomed weight of him. The fullness that she'd somehow never expected but which now made perfect sense.

Cautiously, she breathed deep. Her muscles relaxed a little more. Again his fingers brushed her hair back, then lingered to caress her cheek, lips and throat. By the time he lifted his hand she was arching up, eager for that hand on her breast. He obliged, gently squeezing there, and a little sizzle of excitement shot through her.

'You should have told me.'

Eva didn't want to talk about it. She just wanted this, him. Them. For now, her body had relaxed, and this no longer felt like an impossible burden but a potent promise of pleasure.

'Shh.' She put her fingers to his mouth, tracing those beautifully sculpted lips. Something rose inside her. The familiar welling of love and with it the need for him.

Raking her fingers through his hair, she drew his head down, lifting her other hand up to clutch his shoulder.

Then, everything changed as Paul began to move slowly, cautiously, but even so she felt the phenomenal power of them together. Her untried body responded with a tentative tilt of the hips that made him sink deeper, touching a spot that sent sheet lightning blasting through her.

There was a hiss of breath and Eva realised it came from Paul. She was so wrapped up in wonder at new sensations as they moved together, still slowly, but with increasing confidence. They were like two halves of a whole, melding then almost separating, only to join again in a way that made even the orgasm he'd given her seem insignificant.

Because now they were one, sharing the same ripples of delight, so closely joined it seemed impossible they'd ever again be two separate people.

Eva's heart ached with the beauty of it. She revelled in the husky, velvet undertone of Paul's deep voice, so deep now she barely heard it, but rather felt it like an approving rumble shuddering through her.

His hands were gentle, his mouth on hers deliciously languorous, enticing her to open wide and share all that she was. Meanwhile that honed, lean, powerful body moved with her, drawing her away from everything she'd known and up into the starlit night.

She wanted to sigh at the beauty of it but the tempo of their coupling quickened and she had no breath to spare. Little explosions of excitement began to prickle her body, from her scalp to her soles and everywhere in between.

Her toes curled and she locked him close, hanging

on as their rhythm disintegrated into a pounding, desperate rush.

'Eva!' Her name on his lips sounded beautiful.

But she had no time to concentrate on that as he bit down on the sensitive spot where her shoulder curved up to her neck, and a shot of electric energy tore through her. Paul's hand slid between them, unerringly locating that sensitive nub and pressing hard as he powered hard and fast into her, again and again and again.

It was too much, even though she didn't want it ever to end. Eva felt the flex of his powerful thighs against hers, his glutes bunch hard and a vibration begin in his body and end in hers.

The shaft of pleasure from their joining was so intense, so profound, it obliterated all else.

She heard a shout of triumph, felt heat consume her and then she was lost in a whirl of ecstasy.

When a lifetime later she floated back to earth to find herself sprawled across Paul's damp, heaving chest, she couldn't stop the smile that curved her lips.

That had been the single most wonderful experience of her life.

She and Paul together... Hadn't she known they were made for each other?

Eva lay where she was, her ear pressed to his chest, inhaling the rich, spicy scent of him. Slowly her breathing evened out and her racketing pulse returned to something like normal, but her arms and legs remained boneless. Never mind. She didn't ever want to move.

Except slowly, finally, her brain began to work. To register more than the aftermath of intoxicating pleasure.

That was when her skin began to chill.

Not just her skin, but her blood too.

For, held in Paul's loose embrace, plastered to his magnificent body, her own still humming with the joy he'd given her, she realised the huge mistake she'd made.

She'd loved him since she was fifteen. Had been overwhelmed by hurt and dismay when he'd told her he didn't want her in his life. But instead of walking away with her head up she'd proved just how desperate she was for him. She'd come on to him *even though he didn't want her*.

He might have called out her name as he'd climaxed but he'd only come to bed with her because he'd been primed for sex. Any woman would have done. And this way he hadn't broken his promise to be faithful to his fiancée.

Tonight had changed her life. Yet for Paul it had simply been a convenient and welcome release from celibacy.

That wasn't the worst, though.

Her breath backed up in her lungs.

No, worse by far was the realisation she'd only increased the burden she bore.

Loving Paul from afar had been bad enough. But now she'd had a taste of glory. He'd opened her eyes to a world she'd never known. A world not just of sexual delight but of profound joy. She'd been lucky enough to know the wondrous rapture of sharing herself body and soul with the man she loved.

It was a gift some people never knew. She supposed she should be grateful.

But this gift came at an unbearable cost. It would make leaving, never to see him again, so much more difficult than she'd believed possible even a few short hours before. Because she knew now what she'd be missing.

Eva stared dry-eyed across the room and wished with her whole heart that she'd never laid eyes on Paul of St Ancilla.

CHAPTER SEVEN

SHE WAS STILL asleep when he came back from the bathroom.

As they'd lain entwined in each other's arms, he'd spoken her name and brushed the hair gently from her cheek, but she hadn't responded.

Paul had been almost certain she was awake. She'd held herself so still.

He'd opened his mouth to quiz her then shut it again. He had so many questions, but perhaps this wasn't the time, no matter that his curiosity was insatiable.

How she'd come to be a virgin at twenty-four.

Why tonight she'd suddenly let him past that rigid wall of reserve.

Whether she regretted what they'd done.

He'd drawn in a slow breath and remained silent. No, he was happy to wait for her answer on that one.

Soon after her body had softened against him, her breathing slowing, and he'd known she was indeed sleeping.

He'd waited a little then had gone to dispose of the condom. Now, back in the bed, he lay close enough to feel her warmth, but didn't touch her.

Because if he did there'd be precious little thinking done. Sex with Eva had been phenomenal. He tried to tell himself it was because he'd abstained for so long. It was true he felt a strange, muted triumph at being Eva's first lover, but until now he'd sought experienced partners. If she'd said she was inexperienced, he wouldn't have touched her.

Yeah, right. You'd never have been able to resist. Just looking at her in that short dress drove you to the brink.

A shudder passed through his sated body as he recalled Eva in that slinky dress. He felt a tightening in his groin. A feather of arousal skimmed his spine as she shifted beside him and he inhaled her delectable scent: hot, sexy woman with an intriguing hint of spring flowers.

Even her long hair, almost waist-length, was seductive. The way she looked with it down around her shoulders, her pert breasts peeping out from beneath the silky curtain. The feel of it caressing his flesh as he moved against her.

Gritting his teeth, Paul rolled away and stared towards the window. Already dawn was coming. He saw the first glow of morning.

It was far too soon. He needed to think, and fast. Because dealing with Eva had just got incredibly complicated.

He'd planned to give her her freedom. Except she didn't seem to want it. Now, if he was truthful, letting her walk away held precious little appeal. The way they'd been together…

He drew a slow breath and tried to concentrate. Not

on sex. Not on the physical presence of the woman in bed with him. But on what to do now their relationship had exploded into something completely unrecognisable.

Eva had always been an enigma, apparently docile and always agreeable but never allowing any degree of intimacy. Until tonight. She'd been anything but docile. She'd proceeded to blow the back right off his skull with her sexy mouth and eager hands, reducing him to slavering desperation. Not once but twice.

And she'd been a virgin!

How much more dangerous would she be with a bit more experience?

Paul shuddered and tried to tell himself it was in dismay, not anticipation.

Despite his agitated thoughts, a mighty yawn cracked his jaw as a second night without sleep caught up with him.

The night before the ball he'd pulled an all-nighter, recalibrating the plans his advisers and his brother-in-law, Jake—a financial guru—had devised to keep St Ancilla afloat.

Years of hard work, refinancing and ruthless expenditure-cutting meant the economy hadn't collapsed on itself after King Hugo's depredations. But it was still a close thing. Made particularly difficult as the full extent of those debts, which Paul had personally shouldered, wasn't publicly known. The monarchy was the mainstay of the small kingdom and he had no intention of allowing public confidence to unravel. The good news was that, after coming close to bankruptcy, things were finally turning around.

Paul sighed and closed his eyes for a moment. Just a moment, while he pondered this latest challenge in an already demanding kingship. How to deal with his feisty, surprising fiancée.

Eva smiled and stretched. She felt oh, so warm and cosy. This was the softest bed she'd slept in and she was only too happy to sink into it, not wanting to stir.

Strange. Normally she was a morning person, awake early and full of energy. But not now. She could stay here for ever. She'd never felt so good.

Except for that curious sensation between her legs and…

Her eyelids snapped open. She found herself staring at bright sky through a canopy of spring leaves. She frowned. This wasn't her bedroom. It looked as if she was in a tree house or…

Movement behind her cut off her thoughts.

Heat, searing but delicious, right up against her body. The slide of muscled, hairy legs behind her thighs. A callused palm grazing across her hip to settle at her naked waist, a powerful arm roping her to the man behind her.

Paul!

The hunting lodge.

Their naked bodies moving together. Climaxing as one.

Eva shut her eyes, trying to regroup from the onslaught of memories. But remembering didn't help. It merely heightened her panic.

Her heart thumped so high against her ribs, it felt as if it were trying to escape through her throat.

But it wasn't merely panic she felt, was it? She made no attempt to pull away from him.

'You're awake.' Before last night she'd had no notion Paul could sound like this. Like a lazy lion growling out his satisfaction.

Except, as his rod slid up against her buttocks, hard and powerful, she knew he was anything but lazy, and nowhere near satisfied.

A strange little jiggle set up inside her. A dancing, twisting sensation that felt far too much like eagerness. Because she'd learned last night how very, very good it was when Paul's voice grazed that particular low note across her skin. Almost as good as the feel of him deep inside her or—memory hit with a shudder of delight— kneeling before her, caressing her with his mouth.

Eva opened her lips to speak but whatever she'd been about to say disintegrated on a sigh as he cupped her breast, his hard fingers exquisitely gentle.

'You like that.' Another rumble of that deep voice. This time she felt the words as puffs of hot air stirring the hair at her nape. He leaned in and nuzzled her there, his muscled chest at her back.

'So do you.'

His erection felt huge. Had she really accommodated all that last night? A shivery feeling began at what she guessed was her womb then radiated through her whole body.

'You're right. I do.' His teeth grazed her neck and Eva arched back, like a bow strung tight, breast pushing into his palm, backside rubbing against his erection. It was totally instinctive, unplanned, and part of her despaired that she had so little resistance. Until she heard Paul's guttural murmur against her skin, felt his matching thrust against her and knew she wasn't the only one acting on pure instinct.

'I want you, Eva.'

His voice had the roughened richness of whisky and it did terrible things to her brain. Even so, she had just enough sense of self-preservation left to remember that sex with Paul was no good for her. No matter how good it felt.

She swallowed, about to tell him she wasn't interested, when his palm left her breast and arrowed down over her belly, straight to the core of her. His hand settled there as if it belonged, sliding against dampness, easily insinuating to the very spot where...

Her view of leaves and sunlight blurred as her body jerked against his touch.

He kissed her shoulder. 'Hold that thought.' Then, before she could respond, he was gone. She heard the rustle of foil behind her and realised he was getting a condom.

Now was the time to move. To think with her brain, not her body, and get up.

She'd actually put her hand on the mattress, about to lever herself off the bed, when he spoke behind her. 'You're not sore? I've never been with a virgin. I don't want to hurt you.'

Eva paused, her heart squeezing. She told herself it made no difference that Paul was concerned about her. That he wasn't totally driven by his own carnal needs.

Yet it did make a difference.

'Eva? You *are* okay, aren't you?' He was close again,

capturing some of her hair and drawing it aside to reveal one side of her face and a shoulder.

There it was again. Concern. Caring. Her well being mattered to him.

Yeah, because when he washes his hands of you he doesn't want any excuse to feel bad.

Strangely, the bitter thought didn't overwhelm her. Instead it made her feel stronger.

At least she knew exactly what she meant to him. She wasn't his possession, or his responsibility. She was an independent woman and could choose as she wished, do what she wished.

Sternly, she banished the voice that told her being intimate with Paul would only make things harder to bear later. She'd worry about later when it came. After all, the damage was already done. Why not do what he did and enjoy the moment?

'Of course I'm okay. I'm not a porcelain doll.'

Even so, for the longest time he didn't move. She felt him watching her, staring at her profile, as if searching for some sign that she wasn't okay at all.

Briefly, the thought entered her head that she should turn to him and tell him how she felt. That, at least, would solve the issue of keeping her distance from him so as to avoid more hurt. Because hearing a declaration of love would be guaranteed to cool his ardour. But, perversely, Eva didn't want him to pull back. Her need for him was stronger, not weaker.

Even her anger at him for not reciprocating her feelings only served to fuel her need.

So, instead of turning her head to look up at the man peering over her shoulder, Eva arched her back again so her buttocks pushed against hard male flesh and she heard his rough intake of breath.

Triumph filled her. In this at least she had power. She felt it thrum through her as his hand clutched convulsively at her hip and his body slid against hers.

Tentatively she wriggled her hips, as if getting more comfortable on the bed, and was rewarded with something that sounded like a groan.

'Unless you're not up to it,' she purred, gaze focused on the flickering leaves beyond the window. 'I'll understand if you feel too tired.'

Paul growled something under his breath. Something gruff and low. Then his hand moved from her hip to other, far more sensitive places and Eva lost any interest in talking.

This time their coupling was so easy, it amazed her. Not only was there no pain but it seemed so simple, so right, even that first thrust stole her breath. The perfection of them moving together, finding their rhythm, dazzled her.

Paul was still behind her when she felt his climax begin. She stared blindly in the direction of the tree tops outside. Yet in her mind's eye it was Paul she saw, his strong throat arching as he shouted his release, his eyes glittering like dark sapphires.

A sob broke from her throat, her heart aching. He was the man for her, the only one she'd ever wanted. That thought and the ache it brought died as with one final surge he drew her down into rapturous pleasure.

Eva's orgasm was drawn out, lingering and potent. She had no doubt what made it so amazing was the fact she shared it with the man she loved. That was the definition of bliss.

Finally, they lay together, quaking yet boneless. As the rapture faded, she felt a tear track across her cheek.

She didn't raise a hand to wipe it away. She didn't have the energy. And Paul wouldn't notice. He lay spooned behind her, his face buried in her hair.

Well, what was one tear? She'd permit herself that single sign of weakness. After this there'd be no leeway. She couldn't afford any slip-ups that might betray her true feelings.

She'd be dry-eyed and completely controlled when they separated.

It was late when Paul finally roused again. He peered out at the lowering sky and steady drizzle and wondered how long he'd slept.

Two nights with little sleep had caught up with him. And a couple of stupendous climaxes. He yawned and tried to focus. He hadn't meant to sleep again. Even in this grey light he could tell the day was well advanced.

He turned his head to see if Eva was awake, only to discover the bed empty.

He shot up, heart thumping.

One thing he'd learned last night was never again to take Eva for granted. Far from being predictable, she'd turned his world on its head in less than a day.

A second later he was on his feet, prowling the room. There were his clothes, flung anyhow across the floor. But not Eva's.

Paul swung his head round, peering into corners, but

found nothing. Not a trace of her. The open door to the bathroom showed she wasn't there.

His gut clenched in a way that told its own story. Concern, annoyance and something like fear brewed deep inside.

Where had she gone? They needed to talk, now more than ever. Important issues were in the balance. Besides, he realised, raking his hand across his scalp, he needed to make sure she was okay.

Inevitably his gaze trailed back to the bed and the small but telling spot on the rumpled sheet. A reminder, as if he needed it, that he hadn't merely taken a lover last night. He'd deflowered a virgin. While Eva had seemed fine earlier this morning—more than fine, in fact—he couldn't kick the concern weighing on him. She'd been as enthusiastic as him for morning sex but was she now regretting it?

Where was she?

The woman he'd once thought he knew had changed. There was no saying what she'd do or where she was. Maybe she'd gone, leaving him behind as she'd done last night, heading off alone and unprotected for that nightclub.

The thought made his hackles rise and every protective instinct kick in.

A second later he was taking the stairs two at a time.

He found her in the kitchen, barefoot and wearing the short, satiny dress that clung to her curves.

Paul swallowed and stopped in the doorway.

She stood at the coffee machine. It was a large commercial-grade one but she looked as at home as she did gracing a royal ball.

Her hair was up, but not in its usual, almost severe style. It was bunched up loose and low, looking as if one quick tug would make it tumble free.

Paul had instant recall of the texture of those long tresses against his skin. He'd never made love to a woman with hair like Eva's. Hadn't realised how incredibly alluring those long swathes of silk could be.

He drew a sharp breath, pungent with the aroma of fresh coffee and the lingering scent of Eva.

Hell! They needed to have a serious discussion, and here he was, imagining her naked in bed with him. Or not even naked. Memory hammered into him of Eva on that huge, scrubbed wooden table, her thighs warm around him, her head flung back and breasts thrusting forward as she rode out the orgasm he'd given her. So beautiful. So...

'Paul!'

She swung round, a cup in her hand, and was staring at him as if she'd never seen him.

If he'd hoped for a smile or any sort of welcome he was doomed to disappointment. His lover—his *lover.* Satisfaction stirred at the thought—was frowning as if wondering why he was here.

Pushing back his shoulders, Paul sauntered into the kitchen, the old flagstones smooth beneath his feet.

'That smells amazing. Can you make me some too?'

For a moment she didn't speak, just stared at him with wide eyes the colour of the wintry sky outside.

And hello to you too.

It had been a long time since Paul had done a morning-after but he recalled them being a whole lot more affectionate than this. Eva looked at him as if he were something conjured from a nightmare.

Except… Her gaze skittered from his, down, a long way down, then up again, slowly. The tip of her tongue caught at the corner of her mouth and her nostrils flared as she breathed deep.

When she met his eyes again, she looked a little dazed. Or was that masculine ego talking? He almost forgave her for that initial horrified look.

He covered the rest of the space between them to stand a breath away from her. She smelt like coffee and that distinctive green floral scent of hers. And the memory of rapture.

A frisson of arousal shuddered through him and he contemplated deferring chitchat for something more satisfying.

'Of course.' Her voice was crisp, at odds with the expression on her face. 'I'll make it while you get dressed.' Her gaze dropped as far as his shoulders then quickly rose.

'That's okay. I'll wait for it. Besides, we have things to discuss.'

Because those furtive glances gave the lie to her tone. She might want to pretend nothing had happened between them but Paul refused to let her retreat again, acting as if they were no more than polite strangers. He'd stop her from re-erecting those barriers if he had to stand here, naked, for the next hour.

She swallowed, and abruptly she didn't look distant but vulnerable.

'I'd prefer it if you were dressed.' Her breath was a barely audible sigh. 'You're too distracting like that.'

'Good.' He leaned down and brushed her lips with his, then lingered as he tasted her. His hand lifted to her cheek, his knuckles sliding down soft flesh.

'Careful!' She jerked back. 'I don't want to spill coffee on you. Really, you should get dressed.'

Her gaze left his face and focused on his groin where, even after their earlier, vigorous activity, his burgeoning interest was evident.

Paul's mouth curved. That was better. Eva looked anything but distant now. Her eyes were round and her lips parted. She looked adorable.

'On one condition.' Her head jerked up and their gazes meshed. 'That when I come back downstairs you stop trying to put up barriers between us. We need to talk frankly with each other, Eva. No holding back. No pretending last night didn't happen. Okay?'

She hesitated then nodded. 'Okay.'

Paul turned and strode to the door, giving Eva a perfect view of his muscled back and taut glutes. Even after last night's intimacies, she was stunned by the sight of him naked.

It was a sight she was pretty sure she'd carry for the rest of her days.

Eva put her coffee down with a hand that trembled and turned on the tap, putting her wrists under the flow of cool running water, then lifting them to her cheeks. Heat had bloomed inside the instant he'd appeared stark naked and overwhelmingly, stunningly gorgeous.

Paul didn't fight fair. Standing there looking like... like...

She shook her head and gave up trying to think of

a word. When she'd turned round and seen him in the doorway, her brain had emptied. When she'd recovered it was to the realisation that making love to him had indeed left her more vulnerable than ever before.

He'd been semi-erect again, and she'd been torn between fascination and horror at the messages her traitorous body sent to her brain. To forget pride and common sense, and the fact that he didn't want her long term, and offer herself to him again. Even though she needed to break her ties to him, not make them stronger.

She closed her eyes, trying and failing to banish the image of that powerful body and potently attractive grin.

He was incredibly sexy, yet it wasn't just that. Her hormones responded predictably to the picture he presented, all virile male, but she'd noticed something more than invitation in his expression. He was concerned about her.

Eva firmed her lips. The last thing she needed was for him to come over all honourable and worried about the fact she'd been a virgin. She might long for him with all her heart but last night had seen a shift in her. Better, she realised now, to move on than stay with a man who'd never reciprocate her feelings.

Straightening from the sink, she took out another cup and turned to the coffee machine.

They'd have the discussion he wanted.

She'd agree to end the engagement, stay while they sorted out a suitable press release then return home.

And do what?

Stunned, she stood frozen as revelation sank into her. She'd thought for so long that she was destined to be

Queen of St Ancilla. Even the university degree she'd completed hadn't been done with the aim of securing herself a job. Her job was supposed to be supporting Paul and the people of St Ancilla. She'd been trained from birth to be a royal, to serve a nation. As a teenager she'd thought of a career, but after her betrothal had thought that that was impossible.

Now it wasn't only possible. It was vital.

What would she do with her life? She couldn't see herself returning to Tarentia to live in her parents' shadow for ever.

She had to start thinking of the future. A future away from St Ancilla, though she'd come to love the place. A future where she worked at something other than being royal.

Eva clutched at the kitchen bench, for a moment overwhelmed by the enormous changes she faced.

But this was a positive. She could build a career and be independent, not tied to the royal court, always living up to impossibly high expectations.

She just had to decide what that future would be. Hopefully something fulfilling. Something where she could make a difference.

Footsteps descending the staircase cut through her thoughts and she moved to the coffee machine. It was easier to focus on making a perfect espresso than grapple with the issue of her future. There'd be plenty of time once she left here. An endless lifetime ahead without Paul.

Don't think like that.

Think of this as an opportunity. Think about the free-

dom to work at something you enjoy. The freedom and independence.

Her nape prickled. Paul had arrived. Her body always told her when he was looking at her.

Straightening her shoulders, she practised a nonchalant smile. All she had to do was agree on how they were going to break the news of their split and she could leave.

She ignored the cramping pain through her middle.

'Here.' She turned, that small smile pinned to her face. 'Just the way you like it.'

She held out his coffee but Paul ignored it. Slowly he looked up from his phone. His brow was crunched in a scowl that drew his eyebrows close. Deep lines cut around his mouth and his jaw looked as if it was carved of granite.

'Paul? What is it?' Her heart leapt. 'Bad news?'

Belatedly he reached out and took the cup, only to place it on the table beside him.

He pulled a chair from the table for her. 'You'd better sit down.'

He must have read her sudden fear for he shook his head and his mouth curved ever so slightly. 'Don't worry. It's not bad news from Tarentia. Your family is fine.'

His eyes cut to his phone. 'But we have a problem.'

CHAPTER EIGHT

EVA WATCHED PAUL take the chair next to hers. 'Tell me.'

His dark-blue eyes bored into hers. There was nothing lover-like about his gaze now. Though there was concern. 'Last night. That scene behind the night club.' His mouth hooked down at the corners. 'It's all over social media and the press.'

'I don't understand.' But that was just her brain rejecting his words. Looking into his grim features, Eva understood this was all too real.

'You were right about others being in the vicinity when you went out the back door. Someone had a phone and used it to snap a photo.'

'Of you fighting?'

Eva recalled Fabrice's hot breath and grasping hands. His heavy weight against her. His violent snarl as he'd promised retribution for that knee to the groin. She'd been so thankful when Paul had ripped him off her. She wasn't a fan of violence but in the circumstances she could feel nothing but gratitude and relief that he'd intervened. But a shot of the king brawling in a back alley would be a PR nightmare, even though he'd been saving her.

Paul shook his head. 'No. The photo is of you and him up against the wall.'

Bile rose at the thought. It was bad enough to live with the vivid recollection, to feel that phantom clutch of greedy hands and the slide of those wet lips. But to have others *see* what had happened...

Eva's shoulders hunched as she pulled her arms in tight against her body. She felt grubby, tainted. It did little good to say *she'd* done nothing wrong. That it was Fabrice who should feel shame. But, despite logic, something deeper and more primitive scoured through her. She didn't want to hear this. Even more, she didn't want everyone else to know about it.

'So the press are reporting the attack.' She told herself it would be a nine-day wonder. That after the initial flurry of interest it would be forgotten.

'Not exactly.'

She looked up sharply and didn't like the expression she saw on Paul's face. Anger but something else she couldn't name. 'What?'

'There's only one photo and it's of *you*. You and...'

'Fabrice,' she said through clenched teeth. Was that even his real name?

'Fabrice.' He leaned back in his seat, as if getting more comfortable, except every line of his rigid body spoke of tension. 'The story splashed everywhere is that you were making out with him willingly. That, far from wanting me to interrupt, you were planning to go off with him to...'

Something jammed high up in Eva's chest as if someone had stuck a knife between her ribs, catching her lungs in the process so she couldn't breathe.

Finally, she forced out the words. 'Say it.'

Serious eyes held hers and now the expression she read there was overwhelmingly of sympathy.

'To have sex. Apparently you were on the prowl, looking for a one-night stand, until I came and butted in. The stories about what happened next are sketchy, presumably because there aren't photos. In some versions there was a fight. In others I simply grabbed you and marched you back to the palace.'

Pain banded Eva's torso. Breathing actually hurt.

How could that be, when she knew full well the media's ability to turn the most innocent glance into something totally different? The press spun stories out of air, inventing feuds, rivalries, love stories and so much more. Not that she'd been a particular victim.

But this… Turning the most shocking, frightening experience of her life into salacious gossip for the masses… She pressed her hand to her stomach, clamping her lips shut as nausea hit.

'Here.' Eventually she heard Paul's voice, soft near her ear. He wrapped her hand round a glass. Eva looked down and saw she held a half-full glass of water, its surface rippling as her hand shook.

'Thanks.' She sipped it, forcing the liquid down her constricted throat. That gave her something to focus on other than the raging whirl of emotions inside.

Putting down the glass, she held out her hand for his phone. 'Show me.'

Hers was still in the small bag she'd taken with her last night and the battery was flat.

'I don't think you really—'

'No, I'm sure I don't want to see what they say.' Determined, she held his gaze. 'But I need to. Please.'

Reluctantly, he placed in on her palm. Her fingers closed round it tentatively, as if it might bite. Her mouth curled in a bitter smile. It was too late to worry about getting hurt. The damage was done.

Even so, the next five minutes were a test of her endurance. Her stomach curdled as she read the stories and speculation about her. When she saw the photo, her stomach cramped so hard she thought she'd vomit.

From this angle you couldn't tell the embrace was forced. It was obvious he'd kissed her and the position of his groping hand at her breast was revoltingly clear.

Her hand was up against his shoulder. Eva recalled shoving with all her might. But that could look as though she'd clung for support.

The shot was taken from one side. Fabrice's face was unclear but the side of Eva's face was in focus, including one of the distinctive sapphire earrings she'd worn to the ball that night. And, if there'd been any doubt about her identity, the engagement ring Paul had given her was there for all to see. A pear-shaped blue diamond. It was truly distinctive.

A shudder passed through her then she gave the phone back to him and got up, collecting both his coffee cup and hers.

'Where are you going?' Instantly Paul was beside her.

Did he think she was going to storm off?

And do what? Track down Fabrice, whose surname she didn't even know, and force him to admit what had happened?

Complain to the press?

Rant on social media?

Eva breathed deep and tipped the cold coffee out of the untouched cups.

'To make us fresh coffee.' She didn't need the caffeine. She already had so much adrenaline storming through her bloodstream, she'd be wired for the rest of the day. But it gave her something to do.

'I'm sorry about this, Eva.'

'It's not your fault.' She sent him a sideways glance, noting the harsh set of his steely jaw.

'It is. I should have thought about photos. But all I could focus on was making you safe and getting you away from there.'

Eva concentrated on measuring the ground coffee. 'And I'm grateful.'

She couldn't let herself dwell on how she felt right now. Or on the temptation to seek comfort in his arms.

From the corner of her eye she saw him rake his hand through his hair. The gesture pulled his thin sweater taut across his chest and her breath snagged. Not in distress but appreciation.

Her emotions were all over the place. If Paul turned to her now, took her hand and whispered seduction in her ear, she'd follow him back up the stairs to that round tower-room and let his loving push all this grimy gossip from her mind.

He didn't.

Of course he didn't.

'We'll deal with this, Eva. Don't fret.'

She shot him a stunned glance, then realised she

shouldn't be surprised. Paul had a protective streak a mile wide and a well-honed sense of responsibility.

But Eva was no longer his responsibility.

'You don't need to get involved. I'll handle it once I'm gone.'

'Gone?'

She frowned, her thoughts on what she had to do next.

Eva handed him his tiny cup and picked up her own, sniffing the rich aroma, telling herself she'd feel stronger once she'd drunk it.

'Once I'm in Tarentia. We're no longer engaged, remember?'

For a second he stood motionless, regarding her. Then he lifted the cup and drank, not even grimacing as he swallowed the scalding hot coffee.

He half-turned to put his cup down then faced her again, the picture of assured, powerful male. To her dismay, Eva really did feel tempted to lean against that broad shoulder and let him take charge.

'You're upset, and that seems to have affected your memory. Fortunately, I have perfect recall. I raised the possibility of breaking our engagement and you didn't like the idea. We agreed to discuss it today.'

'Okay, we'll discuss it now.' She sipped her coffee, willing the warm liquid to make her feel stronger. 'I agree that we should end the engagement. It's sensible for us to split up.'

A half-smile hooked up the corner of Paul's mouth. Despite the sick feeling lurking in her stomach, his smile sent delicious warmth cascading through her.

As if they were still upstairs in bed and the only thing on their minds was sex.

'I disagree.'

'You what? It was your idea!' She felt her eyes round as she stared up at him. She'd never seen Paul look quite so...immoveable. But then she'd never taken an opposing position to him before. Until last night.

Eva took in his widened stance, crossed arms and a glint in his eyes that signalled his intention to be very obstinate indeed.

'Now, more than ever, we need to stick together.' He spoke softly but his voice hit a low register that gave his words gravitas. As if his decision was best and there could be no reasonable argument.

Eva shook her head at his stubbornness. She took a sip of coffee, searching for the words she needed to end this once and for all.

'You can't afford the scandal, Paul. I know you've worked hard to put on a good front for the public. That you want to avoid anyone digging too deep into the royal family's doings because they might uncover your father's crimes. It makes sense to end this now, before the media storm gets worse.'

If Paul had looked obstinate and half-amused before, that expression vanished as he frowned.

'You think *that's* what motivates me? Fear of scandal?'

Eva's brow puckered. That was what her father had said and it made sense, given what she'd heard about King Hugo's involvement in fraud and outright theft from the public purse.

'There are reasons I preferred that the press didn't

run with the full details of my father's crimes at the
time. St Ancilla's finances were seriously compromised.
A fortune in investment funds was squandered on the
turn of a roulette wheel, money that should have gone
into social development projects. Meanwhile, more public funds were syphoned off to cronies.'

A tic started up in the vein at his temple, something
she'd never seen before.

'Since then we've worked hard to refinance, attract
additional investors and begin, slowly, to make good
the losses. Because if the bare facts had been known
earlier it would have caused such loss of confidence,
the nation itself might have been in peril.' He drew a
breath that made that broad chest rise.

'For major investors and many of our citizens, the
royal family *is* St Ancilla. That's why the full details
haven't yet become public. So we could keep afloat long
enough to be viable again.'

'I'm not accusing you of anything.' He had too much
integrity. She knew he wasn't tainted by his father's
activities.

Paul shook his head and his dark hair flopped down
across his forehead, making Eva's fingers twitch with
the urge to reach out and brush it back. It made him
look less daunting and even sexier, despite the simmering indignation in his eyes. Instead she moved to put
her cup down.

'But you think I'm running scared of negative publicity.' His stare bored into hers and heat drilled through
her.

'I don't give a damn about protecting my father's
reputation. I only want to make good what he and his

cronies took. We've had a team of forensic accountants and investigators tracking money and preparing briefs of evidence that will go to court soon. It's taken years of complex investigations to get the necessary evidence.' He shrugged. 'And I'm not saying we're out of the woods yet, financially, but things are better than they were.'

'I had no idea.'

'Why should you? We don't discuss financial matters.'

We don't discuss anything important. We don't have that kind of relationship.

Or, they hadn't. It felt as if last night had changed that.

Paul spread his hands in a gesture that invited trust. 'If you think for a second I'd abandon you now when you need me, just to avoid bad publicity, then you don't know me at all.'

'It sounds,' she said slowly, thinking things through, 'that bad publicity is going to hit your family when the court cases start anyway.'

He shrugged. 'So be it. Crimes were committed and have to be dealt with. Sweeping it under the carpet isn't a long-term option. As for the publicity, it's nothing I can't handle. My siblings aren't even in the country and my mother is retired from public life, living in France.'

So the decks were cleared. The one who'd face the media storm would be Paul. He had it all worked out.

Something about his expression gave Eva pause, her mind ticking over.

Had this been a factor in him wanting to end their engagement? He'd said he wanted to make good the dowry money his father had already spent. Had he also planned to ensure Eva wouldn't be caught up in negative publicity around the St Ancillan royal family?

She opened her mouth to ask then shut it again. Maybe he simply didn't want to marry her. Didn't like her enough to spend the rest of his life with her. She felt bruised enough without making him say that to her face.

Eva shrugged. 'I applaud what you're doing, Paul. I'm impressed.' Doubly so because, despite his talk of an international team, she guessed he was the one driving the process. A man who'd inherited the crown in his early twenties and who'd had to manage incredibly difficult challenges, learning as he went. He had enough to contend with.

'But you don't need this.'

'No buts, Eva. We're in this together. The worst, the absolute worst, thing we could do right now is end our engagement. People would think it confirmed the stories being circulated about you.'

'What if I say I don't care what people say? Bad publicity isn't the end of the world.'

Paul reached out and took her hand. Funny, she hadn't realised she was cold till she felt his warm fingers enfold hers. She didn't even try to tug free. His touch was so comforting.

'I'd say you haven't thought through how bad it can be. That one photo can taint you for ever.'

His words shafted ice through her. Eva knew she could face what she had to, but it wouldn't be pleasant. The idea of one incident being misinterpreted and haunting her for the rest of her days made her nauseous.

'We stick together, Eva. We don't give the story any oxygen. It's the only way. Surely you see that?'

Still she hesitated. Instinct told her that, if she was going to break this engagement, the sooner the better. Her emotions were tangled enough already.

She shook her head. 'It's not up to us. The story will run, no matter what we do.'

His hand tightened on hers. 'But it will run its course faster if you stay here in St Ancilla, at my side. If we're seen spending time together, enjoying each other's company.'

'You mean, if you're seen to trust me.'

'Exactly.' His expression grew more serious. 'Please, Eva, let me do this for you.'

Eva sighed, her breath shuddering out as the fight finally left her.

She didn't have a heavy schedule in Tarentia. She'd finished studying, had thought she'd be busy the next few months preparing for their wedding. A chill enveloped her.

She told herself this was the sensible option. But secretly she wondered if the real reason she wavered was because part of her still hadn't got the message about cutting her ties with Paul.

He stood so near, she inhaled that reassuring scent of pine trees and the outdoors. And his touch, the feel of his fingers wrapped casually around her hand, evoked memories of other more intimate touches.

'Eva?' He bent closer, snagging her attention.

Expelling her breath in a sigh of acceptance, she inclined her head. 'On two conditions.'

One black eyebrow arched high. 'Go on.'

'That this is time-limited.' Stupidly, she felt her throat close on the last word, as if her subconscious didn't want her to make the break from him.

'Fair enough. We'll review the situation in a couple of months.'

Eva frowned. 'One.'

'Not long enough. Two minimum.' He read her expression. 'If we separate too soon, it will have been for nothing. How about we regroup in six weeks and assess how things are? But in that time you stay here in St Ancilla.'

She hesitated. 'Surely me staying here all that time will just raise false expectations?'

'The whole point is for us to be seen as a caring couple, finally free to spend time together now you've finished your studies. What happens later...' he shrugged '...well, that's for later. The point is to show what happened hasn't affected my feelings. That I trust your integrity.'

He was railroading her. Yet what were her options? She shrank from returning home with her tail between her legs, knowing her parents' media advisers would be lumbered with responsibility for fixing this.

Again she told herself the publicity was no big deal. Yet in Tarentia it would be. As far as the public was concerned, she was a bit of a goody two-shoes. Always proper, never putting a foot out of line. Last night's adventure would be fodder for press gossip for a long time to come, and the dissolution of her engagement on top of that... No, she couldn't embarrass her family that way.

'Okay. Agreed.'

Light blazed in his eyes. Triumph or approval?

'Excellent. And the other condition?'

'We handle the media my way.'

CHAPTER NINE

PAUL HAD TO hand it to Eva—she didn't shirk. For a moment yesterday when she'd spoken of handling the media her way he'd wondered if she meant hiding from the press and hoping the negative stories would all go away.

Which was totally ludicrous, if you knew Eva. And he was beginning to know Eva.

In some ways he still had so much to learn about her. In others, he knew Eva very well indeed. The surreptitious thought crept up on him, threatening to unravel his composure as he relived the sweet sound of her climaxing, and the feel of her moving against him. Her movements had been eager, if a little inept, till she'd found her rhythm, and all the more arousing for that.

He concentrated on marshalling his features into a sympathetic expression as he turned from the journalists in front of him to the woman speaking beside him.

Definitely better to look sympathetic than like he was lusting after her. Which he was.

Not just now but ever since she'd kissed him in the kitchen and shattered the sexual barriers between them.

Or maybe earlier. That night, as she'd flounced down

the stairs to the ball looking remote and superior and at the same time too sexy for his equanimity.

He yanked his attention back to what Eva was saying. That women had the right to be unmolested, at night as well as in daylight. That dancing with a man didn't confer sexual rights. That, in hindsight, she'd think twice about accepting at face value a stranger's offer of assistance in locating a taxi. But wasn't that a sad state of affairs?

Pride swelled as he listened. She'd been right to do this herself rather than leave the PR specialists to craft a press release. Eva had a naturalness, a charming approachability, that drew her listeners in and made her moments of gravity all the more profound.

She'd be such an asset at his side long-term. How had he not realised?

But then the only time they'd faced the press together had been on the occasion of their betrothal, each nervous, each aware that the match had been engineered not because of personal preference but for dynastic reasons.

He looked back now and wondered why he'd let her obvious discomfort colour his view of her. He'd been uncomfortable too. His attempt to kiss her had been clumsy and ill-timed. No wonder she'd pulled away.

Not like her kisses now.

Heat brewed deep in his belly.

'And your thoughts, Your Majesty?' He turned to meet the inquisitive stare of a local reporter.

Paul reached out his hand and took Eva's, threading his fingers through hers.

'Frankly, I feel ashamed that this should happen in

St Ancilla. Naturally, at a personal level, my fiancée's distress weighs on me. It's also drawn my attention to the danger any woman can face at any time from predatory men. It's something we're all aware of but too often we—that is, men—forget because we think it doesn't affect us personally.'

Slim fingers squeezed his and warmth shot through him. Not the heat of arousal like before, but something altogether different, yet just as potent. He liked it.

'It does affect us,' he continued. 'Unless we *want* a society where our neighbours, colleagues, sisters, wives and fiancées are potentially under threat.'

'So what do you suggest we do?' asked a man in the second row. 'Are you advocating violence? It's been reported that you brawled with the man.'

Paul felt as much as heard the hush fall across the small crowd of journalists. Eva's hand tightened around his. In warning?

He turned towards her and saw she once again wore what he now thought of as her public face. Her expression was serene, but he knew her well enough now to understand the slightly up-tilted angle of her jaw and the silvery glitter in her eyes. This session was tougher than she was letting on and she was upset, or perhaps worried about where this was leading.

Did she fear charges might be laid against him?

Paul turned back to his questioner. 'I'm not advocating violence. I'm suggesting we all think carefully about our behaviour. About the words and actions we, as a society, want to model for our children, or let pass as acceptable. We should call out bad behaviour rather than pretend that sexist or aggressive comments and actions are a bit of a joke. And of course we should each do our bit to help others feel safe.'

'By beating up transgressors?'

Paul met the journalist's stare. 'I had in mind more positive actions, like group car-pooling after an evening out. Or walking friends home.'

'But you—'

'As for my actions the other night, it's true I intervened. The man sexually assaulted my fiancée and was threatening more violence. I pulled him away from her and when he swung at me, yes, I punched him.'

That was a shortened version of events. The guy hadn't given up quickly and Paul hadn't been in a forgiving mood.

'If the man in question wants to come forward and lay charges against me for defending Princess Eva, I'd welcome that. I'm sure the police will be very interested in interviewing him about the events of that evening. It appears likely he was using a false name, which has hampered attempts to find him.'

He turned to Eva beside him. 'For my part, I don't regret what I did. I just wish I'd been there sooner.'

Eva and Paul left the room while palace staff ushered the journalists out of the palace. Paul still held her hand as he led the way silently away from the public reception rooms and she didn't object. His touch was supportive, understanding, and it helped.

The worst was over.

Hopefully.

She breathed a deep sigh as some of the tension fell away from her stiff shoulders.

Relief filled her, laced with a shot of self-disgust. What had happened to her had been nothing compared with the sexual violence suffered by many other women. It seemed almost self-indulgent to feel so undone, reliving the experience.

'Are you all right?' Paul led her into his study and to a big, leather-upholstered lounge. He drew her down to sit beside him.

'Of course. Don't I look it?'

His mouth quirked in a semi-smile that tugged at her heartstrings. 'You look beautiful, elegant and just a little ruffled.' Then, seeing her dismay, he added, 'No, don't worry. No one else would notice.'

Because he understood her so well he could see what she tried to hide? It was a disturbing idea. As was her reaction to being called beautiful. For too long, she'd craved his interest and approval.

'You did brilliantly, Eva. Reporting of the incident will take a new direction now. One you don't have to worry about.'

She nodded. 'I hope you're right. They seemed to accept the truth, even though a couple of them obviously preferred the original story.'

He shrugged. 'Because it's more scandalous, and scandal sells.'

Eva thought of the report from Paul's security staff. That in the melee, as the security officer had tried to reach her that night, he'd knocked against someone whose phone had dropped and smashed. She didn't ask if that was accidental, just felt relieved there weren't even more photos of the scene.

'Something else is bothering you.'

It wasn't a question but a statement. His perspicacity was scary. For so long she'd prided herself on keeping her emotions hidden from him. If he continued to read her so well, what other things would he uncover?

'Eva?'

She withdrew her hand from his, wondering if it was something about the physical connection that helped him understand her thoughts.

'It's nothing.'

Paul's steady gaze told her he didn't believe it.

She shrugged. 'Just that I feel a bit of a fraud. All this talk about sexual assault when, really, it could have been so much worse.'

'Would you feel better if he'd raped you?'

'Of course not! It's just that, compared with what other women experience... All this fuss is just because I'm newsworthy.' Her stomach gave a nauseating little twist.

He watched her for so long, she wondered what he was thinking.

'You're right. The public attention is because of who you are. But what he did was wrong. A man who thinks he can force himself on a woman is wrong, whether he managed to rape you or grope you or kiss you when you were unwilling.' He paused. 'But, if it's nagging at you, maybe you need to see this as a chance for positive action.'

'Like you did, talking about changing attitudes and behaviour?' His words had resonated. She'd admired him, not because he'd deflected attention from her, but because she could see he meant every word.

'Why not? As you say, you have the public profile

to draw media attention. You could capitalise on that. Use the opportunity to focus public discussion towards change. Every bit helps.'

Slowly, she nodded. 'It's a good idea.' And it would give her something to keep her occupied. Her enforced six-week stay in St Ancilla, longer than any previous visit, stretched ahead without any real plans.

'And Eva?' She met Paul's eyes again and felt a throb of energy pulse through her. 'It *was* sexual assault, and it was inexcusable.'

There it was again, that flash of heat that she'd seen in his eyes when he'd turned to her at the press conference and said he didn't regret fighting her assailant. That he wished he'd got there sooner.

Eva guessed the journalists would take that to mean he wished he'd been there in time to prevent the assault, and she knew that was true. But she also knew, at a primal, bone-deep level, that Paul wished he'd had more time alone with her assailant to make him regret what he'd done.

The realisation should shock her. The civilised woman she was shied from the idea.

But at a deep-seated, not at all civilised level Eva felt jubilation. And excitement. Not at the idea of violence, but because Paul really cared about her. There was no mistaking the emotion in that searing gaze. This wasn't protectiveness because of an arranged betrothal or for the sake of public appearance. This was something primal.

A shiver raced through her, then another, tightening her flesh and making her nipples bud.

For a second, then another, she luxuriated in what

felt like possessiveness. The sort of possessiveness a man felt for his mate.

Then common sense intervened and she tore her gaze away.

She'd had an emotionally draining morning and it had affected her judgement. She was imagining things. Paul didn't regard her as *his*, except in the most temporary way. He'd have done the same for any woman.

For the next month and a half, she had to act the loving fiancée and not read the impossible into Paul's actions when he kept up the same masquerade. Because soon they'd go their separate ways.

Her resolve was tested that very day when he announced they were dining out. Not at a royal function, where she'd be busy making small talk with official guests, but at a private dinner for two.

It would be the first time they'd been alone since they'd left the hunting lodge, except for that brief half-hour following their press conference. For no sooner had they returned to the palace than everyone wanted Paul's attention.

How he'd carved out time for a private dinner, she didn't know. But, despite her nerves at being alone with him again, she was grateful. The St Ancillan palace was comfortable, and the staff eager to please, but it wasn't like being in her own home where she had responsibilities to keep her busy.

Besides, no matter how often she reminded herself their brief period of sexual intimacy must end, she missed him.

They'd had less than twelve hours alone together at the lodge, yet it felt as if everything had changed.

Everything Eva felt for him was intensified. She told herself the idea of a woman fixating on the man who'd taken her virginity was outdated. The trouble was this was no passing sexual obsession. It was just another facet of the love she felt.

The love she had to find a way to conquer.

Even so, she dressed for their dinner date with even more care than when she'd prepared for the royal ball.

She hadn't missed Paul's appreciation of her hair. It had fascinated him when she'd worn it loose. If he hadn't been staring at it he'd been touching it, caressing it with long, slow strokes or wrapping his fists in it, as if to hold her close as they'd crested the wave of rapture together.

Her heart gave a little blip and she decided on impulse to leave her hair loose which she never did for any royal function. Even if they were no longer to be lovers, it didn't mean she could resist the chance to look her best for him.

To show him what he'd miss when he eventually gave her up.

Eva grimaced. Since when had she become petty?

But having the man she loved look at her appreciatively was a temptation too great to be ignored. She brushed her hair till it shone then secured it back on one side with a pearl clip.

Her dress was new, by a designer she'd met on her last visit here. Of pearl-grey chiffon over grey silk, it was embroidered in graduating shades of pink. The colours might be subdued but it fitted like a dream. Its

flirty, floaty skirt made her feel good and the colour
did wonders for her nondescript eyes.

Nevertheless, Eva wasn't prepared for the blatant
admiration in Paul's expression as he met her in the
palace entry hall.

'You look ravishing.' His voice burred to that grav-
elly baritone note that undid something inside her and,
when he lifted her hand to his lips and kissed it, that
sensation of being undone intensified. She had to stiffen
her legs, stand taller in her pale-grey sling-backs and
focus on smiling.

His exaggerated response would be for the benefit of
the footman waiting near the front door, and any other
staff in the vicinity.

'Thank you. You look pretty good yourself.'

In black trousers, a dark jacket that moulded his
straight shoulders and a crisp shirt of palest blue, he
looked good enough to eat.

Heat washed her belly as an image filled her head.
Of her returning Paul's favour and doing to him what
he'd done for her the other night at that big kitchen table.

Lust shuddered through her and she had to fight not
to jump as he reached out and tucked her arm through
his, leading the way outside.

Suddenly it didn't seem such a good idea, wearing
her pretty dress, with her hair down and a new shade
of lipstick she thought made her mouth look appealing.
She'd have been better off in a sombre suit. At least
that would remind her that the night wouldn't end with
them sharing a bed.

Because she couldn't afford sexual intimacy again if

she was going to keep her sanity when the time came to walk away from this engagement.

As for the sideways glance Paul gave her as they descended the steps to his car, that pierced every protective barrier. It was going to take all her determination to keep her distance.

Half an hour later, seated at a discreet table for two on a balcony that hung out over the sea, Eva didn't know whether to laugh or cry. The scene looked like something from a photo shoot of the world's most romantic getaways.

Being here with Paul came heart-achingly close to a parody of what she really wanted from him. Wanted but could never have.

He cared for her, wanted to protect her, had enjoyed sex with her, but he didn't love her. And if he didn't now the chances were he never would.

The sea glimmered below them, indigo shot with the bright colours of the dying sun. Their view down the coast was unparalleled and the restaurant balcony was deserted but for them. Fragrant wisteria spilled down nearby columns, its perfume mingling with sea spice and Paul's warm, outdoorsy scent to create something intoxicating.

Or maybe that was the effect of Paul's dark gaze.

Instead of electric lighting, a myriad of candles in glass holders created an intimate atmosphere.

As for Paul, he looked… No. No more superlatives. She was in deep enough as it was.

'We've never done this before,' she blurted.

His mouth hooked up in a slow smile. If she hadn't

known this date was for show, it would have made her wayward heart hammer even faster than it already did.

'No. That was a definite oversight.'

But totally understandable. Because until now their engagement had been driven by duty and court protocol. Now it was something different. Personal because they'd made it so, yet not a real romance.

The thought dimmed some of the evening's radiance but she countered it with a bright smile.

'So, an unexpected benefit, eh?'

'I hope you'll enjoy it.' His smile reached out to her, as if he really had nothing on his mind but her.

Eva turned to look past him, but realised they were sheltered from view of the diners inside. And, if paparazzi wanted to try to photograph them, they'd have to take a boat off the coast. But then it only took one talkative waiter to spread news of their mood over dinner.

As if conjured by her thoughts, a waiter arrived bearing a platter of appetisers.

When he'd gone, Eva leaned forward, voice low. 'Great choice of venue. We really look like a courting couple out for a romantic interlude.' Hopefully saying it out loud would remind her this was a pretence.

Paul's expression changed. She couldn't define how, just a sense of stillness, almost of wariness.

'You think so?' He reached out and lifted her hand, putting it to his lips, sending a little quake of longing through her. 'I aim to please.'

Yet now she'd swear she read something like annoyance in his features. It didn't make sense.

'There's no need to kiss my hand,' she murmured.

Yet she didn't withdraw. Heaven help her, despite her resolve, breaking physical contact was too tough.

'But you never know,' he said against her knuckles, 'when another staff member might appear. We need to put on a good show.'

Grimly Eva realised there was no need at all for her to act. Being alone with Paul in this beautiful setting, having him focus all his attention on her, elicited the responses she'd tried to hide from him for years. The breathless excitement, hammering heart and dazzled stare.

Eva looked different. Or maybe he just saw things he hadn't noticed in the past. The soft flush of colour high across her cheeks. The invitation of her slightly parted lips. Those tantalising eyes now silver, now misty blue, enticing him.

He closed his hand around hers and placed it on the linen table cloth.

'I'm glad you approve. I've never been here before.' His secretary had said it was the most romantic restaurant in St Ancilla, and Paul had deemed that perfect, because he wanted to reinforce to any interested watchers that they were genuinely romantically involved.

Except now, sitting here with Eva—so alluring— inhaling the gentle drift of hyacinth scent from her warm skin... A tremor raced through him straight to his groin because these days he only had to look at her to want her. His chest felt over-full as he felt her hand shake in his.

Her vulnerability evoked protective instincts. And

possessive ones. That had to be the reason he had trouble focusing on anything but her.

'I have a request.' His voice came out with a curiously raspy edge.

She tilted her head in question, her long hair falling over one shoulder. Paul remembered how it had felt against his bare skin. Soft as silk yet a hundred times more erotic.

He cleared his throat. 'Don't wear your hair down in public.'

'Sorry?' She sat straighter, indignation in that speaking stare.

He felt his mouth curve in an appreciative smile. This was something new. To be attracted to a woman even when she looked annoyed....

Paul leaned in, forcing himself not to lift his other hand to caress her. 'Your hair is incredibly sexy. When I see it down, I have this recurring fantasy about dragging your clothes off and doing things with you that I haven't been able to for a whole day. It's too tempting. Too distracting.' He paused, watching her eyes grow wide. 'Besides, it's unfair on all those other men who will never get the chance to—'

'I get the idea!'

Eva didn't exactly blush but she looked adorably ruffled and Paul wished he hadn't had the brainwave of bringing her here for dinner. An intimate meal in his private apartments would have been so much more comfortable.

And convenient.

But his first consideration was Eva and the need to scotch the speculation about her supposedly wild private life. He'd seen how hurt she'd been by that. He intended to have her by his side as much as possible, giving no one cause to think he had any doubts about her loyalty or her character.

'Paul, we need to talk.' Her gaze flicked past him to the wine waiter returning with drinks.

A few minutes later when they were alone, she said in answer to his question, 'No, not here. It's not private. I'll tell you later.' Then she changed the subject, leaving him curious.

Reluctantly, sensing the subject she deferred was important, he told her about his upcoming schedule and some of the events he thought she might get involved in. His intention was to draw her more into the royal commitments in St Ancilla. It would help rehabilitate her in the eyes of any doubters and, frankly, he'd be grateful for her assistance.

It was fascinating watching her sift through the information he gave her, quickly assessing areas where she could contribute. She was intelligent and had a good appreciation of the work involved even in those events which sounded, to the uninitiated, like mere ceremonial occasions.

Another plus for the dynastic marriage that had been arranged between them. The marriage he'd planned to avoid.

Interesting how that didn't seem such a good idea now.

Eva was born and bred to this work, as was he.

Luckily it seemed her father wasn't the ogre his had been. Failing to live up to King Hugo's expectations had, more often than not, ended with a severe thrashing as well as more devious penalties designed to instil obedience. Was it any wonder Paul had encouraged his younger brothers to go to school out of the country, well away from their father's reach?

The evening passed quickly. He was surprised to discover how late it was when finally he signalled for the bill. From discussing the royal schedule, they'd moved onto his social reform agenda and were soon debating the pros and cons of a number of initiatives.

Paul enjoyed the way Eva was ready to listen to a contrary view and to argue her case. In fact, he intended to refer a couple of initiatives she mentioned to the appropriate staff for further investigation.

All in all, it had been a productive evening. Their dinner out would be reported on and read about by those hungry for signs of a royal split. Eva herself looked so much more relaxed than she had this morning after the press conference.

And now...

He smiled as he helped her into the car then walked around to the driver's seat. Now they had the rest of the night to themselves.

It was only that thought, the promise of Eva's sweet body in his bed later, that had got him through the hours of sitting with her unable to do more than touch her hand.

It had been a revelation, watching her face change as she'd spoken enthusiastically about a project, queried some detail or, occasionally, complimented him on an achievement. Paul hadn't thought himself a vain man but Eva's praise, and the light of approval in her wide eyes, had done crazy things to his ego and his self-control.

He got into the car, strapped on his belt and started the ignition.

'Now, tell me. What was it you couldn't say at the restaurant?' He let out the clutch and the car purred down the long driveway.

Paul looked forward to hearing Eva purr exactly like that, arching under his touch and rubbing herself needily against him. Tonight there'd only be time to do a few of the things he'd been imagining ever since they'd left the seclusion of the hunting lodge. But that would be a start.

Heat stoked deep in his belly and his smile widened. Soon…

'This charade,' she began, then stopped. 'Our engagement.'

'Yes?' Paul's neck prickled. Something in her voice warned him he wasn't going to like this.

'We're going to review the situation in six weeks and decide on the best time to announce we're splitting, right?'

Paul felt an instant protest rise on his tongue and frowned. Six weeks was far too soon to be sure Eva's reputation wasn't damaged. And to put an end to the passionate encounters they'd only just begun.

'Right,' he said slowly.

It was what they'd agreed. No need to say that he was already sure six weeks wouldn't be enough. It had been a tough couple of days for Eva and there was no point getting into an argument about it now. He'd prove to her in the coming month and a half that their engagement should last longer. In fact, all things considered, he was tempted to suggest…

'So I'm only in St Ancilla for a short time before I move on with my life.'

Paul's frown deepened. He didn't like the finality of the picture she was painting. He opened his mouth to respond but she was already speaking.

'In the circumstances, it's better if we don't repeat what happened the other night.' Paul's hands tightened on the wheel and the car veered towards the centre line before he dragged it back. 'We need to keep this as simple and straightforward as possible. I don't want sex with you, Paul. Not tonight. Not ever again.'

CHAPTER TEN

OF COURSE HE tried to change her mind. But once more Eva showed that obstinate streak he'd discovered just a couple of days before.

Nothing he said made a difference. And, as she refused to continue their discussion somewhere private when they returned to the palace, Paul wasn't able to persuade her using more direct methods.

His hands tingled as he considered those direct methods. As he remembered their combustible passion in the few short hours they'd had together. How could she turn her back on what they'd shared? On him?

He spent the night alone in his vast bed, restless and frustrated.

It was amazing how a single night with Eva had shattered his calm, ordered world. True, that night had marked the end of a four-year sexual drought. But surely if he'd mastered anything it was abstinence?

Yet this morning, despite his lack of sleep, he couldn't sit still, as if his body refused to obey the dictates of his mind and focus on work and unrelenting duty. For the first time ever he found it difficult to fix his thoughts on the range of problems and decisions facing him. He spent most of the time pacing his office, alternately hoping Eva had had as little sleep as he, then remembering the weary smudges beneath her eyes as they'd said goodnight and hoping she'd got some rest.

She needed rest. And looking after. And…him.

Silently cursing his circular thoughts, Paul scraped the back of his neck with his palm and turned away from the window.

'The media summary is in, sir.' His secretary appeared in the doorway. Usually the summary of relevant media reports was in by the time Paul reached his office. This morning he'd arrived so early, he'd had to wait.

'And? How bad is it?' Early stories following the press conference had been generally positive, but you never knew for sure.

'Pretty good, considering.'

'Ah.' Considering the inevitable outliers who'd prefer a sensational story to the truth. Paul nodded and returned to his computer, opening the report.

Most of the stories were sympathetic to Eva. There was an editorial about curbing violence against women. Another story used statistics on the number of assault cases in the country in the last year, lower than for many places, but more than anyone wanted.

Then came two, both originating outside St Ancilla, that ran with the 'profligate party girl' theme, trying to paint the picture of a self-absorbed woman whose public face hid a scandalous wild side. Paul wondered how long they'd be able to continue such reporting when they couldn't dredge up any more incidents to support it.

She'd been a virgin till two nights ago.

The knowledge slammed into him like a fist thudding into his temple.

Which was yet another reason why he needed to tread softly now she'd stipulated no sex. Especially after that assault behind the night club.

Both those factors could explain why he felt not only culpable for this furore, but protective.

No, it was more. He felt *possessive*.

Once again Paul rubbed the back of his neck, trying to relieve taut muscles.

He'd never felt this way about any woman.

It must be taking her virginity that explained it.

And the fact that they'd been tied together for four years, even if only via a formal arrangement.

And the fact that he liked her. Admired her.

Was desperate to have her again.

Was that what this was? Thwarted lust?

No, he'd felt proprietorial about Eva when she'd been in his bed.

He gritted his teeth, pain shooting up from his jaw.

'Can I get you anything, sir? A headache tablet?'

Paul shook his head. 'I'm okay, thanks.' Or he would be when he worked out how to deal with his fiancée. 'Give me ten more minutes then bring in the week's schedule, and the Princess's new assistant.'

'My assistant?' Eva stared at the woman before her. Paul *had* been busy. It was only yesterday they'd given their press conference.

'Yes, ma'am. I thought we might begin by mapping out a schedule for you.'

Eva looked at the young woman, only a few years

older than herself, her demeanour serious yet eager. She wanted to warn her that this was only a temporary arrangement. She wouldn't be staying in St Ancilla permanently, so the position of assistant wouldn't be long-term. But, reading her new assistant's enthusiasm, she didn't have the heart. Besides, she and Paul had agreed no one else would know their arrangement was temporary.

She drew a fortifying breath, remembering the scurrilous headlines and the tension in her mother's voice when she'd rung to explain the situation. No, this was the best way forward. It was silly to have second thoughts now.

'Thank you, Helena. That's an excellent idea.'

Helena nodded, passing over a surprisingly large printout.

'I've colour-coded a range of events. Those in gold are ones King Paul thought you could assist him with.'

Obediently Eva scanned the first page. There was at least one gold-shaded event each day, sometimes more. She stifled a sigh. Impossible to expect to avoid him.

She was torn between wanting to be with him and knowing it was best to keep her distance. Being close to him, like on their dinner date last night, made it too easy to forget their relationship had no future.

'As for the others, they're suggestions only, based on my reading of your work in Tarentia and knowing your interest in art and education.'

Eva looked up, surprised.

Helena shrugged. 'I researched you. I know you studied both at university and about your volunteer work in disadvantaged schools.'

'You *are* thorough.' Back in Tarentia, she got press attention when attending royal or high-profile charity events, but her few hours a week volunteering generally went under the radar.

'It's my job. You'll see I've marked those in green.'

'And the blue?'

'Designed to build positively on yesterday's press conference.'

Eva scanned the list.

Visits to a range of groups—including one that provided positive male role models to local kids, a women's shelter and a program designed to help troubled or violent teenagers through sport and learning.

Eva paused then pointed to an hour blocked out this afternoon. 'This isn't colour-coded. Is it a mistake?'

Helena leaned forward. 'No mistake. The King and the press office had a long list of suggestions for your schedule, but I added a few of my own. They're perhaps not so worthy but I think them important.'

She paused. 'His Majesty mentioned you needed to go shopping. I thought you might like to revisit the designer who created the dress you wore last night.'

The dress Paul had so approved of, and which had appeared in various press articles today. Paul had been right. There might not have been paparazzi photographing them while they ate, for which she was thankful, but they'd managed to get quite a few shots of Paul and Eva arriving at and leaving the restaurant.

Eva nodded. A couple more outfits would be good. She'd packed for a week's visit, not for a month and a half, if not more. It wasn't as if she was on a private holiday, not with this schedule. For some of the time, she'd be acting as Paul's proxy. She had to look the part.

Eva nodded. 'I like her designs, plus it would be good to support a local enterprise.'

'Exactly!' Her new assistant gave her a brilliant smile. 'Good press for you and for the designer. It will certainly boost her business, dressing our Queen-to-be.'

Eva's chest cramped on the words but she knew her expression didn't give away her pain. Queen of St Ancilla was something she'd never be.

Once more she felt doubt open up inside her. Surely this schedule would cement her as a fixture in St Ancilla's royalty? Wouldn't that make her eventual split from Paul more difficult?

But to leave now would undo all the good yesterday's press conference had done and she knew Paul would be immoveable. He'd flat-out refuse to end their betrothal yet.

Helena pointed to other appointments squeezed in the schedule. 'This is an old family-run company that makes shoes. It used to be one of St Ancilla's traditional industries but increasingly it's under threat from cheap imports. But their shoes are of excellent quality and I thought...'

Eva laughed. 'So long as they can make more than hiking boots and lace-up brogues, I'll be happy.' Though now she thought about it, she needed a new pair of hiking boots.

'And this one?'

'A lace-making guild.'

'Let me guess. Another traditional industry here?'

Helena spread her hands. 'Why not kill two birds with one stone? You need some clothes and they need—'

'It's fine, Helena. If I can do my bit for local tradition and businesses, I'm happy to help.'

Which was how Eva found her days filled with a schedule even busier than the one she had in Tarentia. At least in Tarentia she knew the place intimately. Here, in Paul's kingdom, she was a newcomer and had to do much more preparation for every engagement.

Despite the years she'd put into studying Ancillan history, politics, geography and language, she didn't feel nearly as confident in saying or doing the right thing.

She relied on Helena and Paul. Inevitably Paul, for she saw him daily, not only during their joint engagements but every evening over dinner and sometimes at breakfast.

Eva tried to keep her distance, not relax in his company or take it for granted, but it was a battle she'd already lost. Keep her distance? Impossible. This strange situation inspired intimacy, created by their common purpose and the secret about their faux engagement.

Yet it would be over soon enough.

That was what Eva told herself constantly but it had little effect. Each day she looked forward to the time she'd be with him. She responded to his easy smile and ready charm. More than once she found herself basking in his approval as he complimented her on how she'd handled some situation. As for those times when he touched her…a hand at her elbow or the small of her back…it took everything she had not to shiver in response and lean into his hand.

She enjoyed those touches too much.

That was why she didn't object when those occasional touches grew more frequent, and not just in public.

Such as now, three weeks after the fateful night of the ball and her disastrous night-club visit.

As she entered the small dining parlour Paul held out a chair for her at the breakfast table and gave her a smile that made her head swim. She'd no sooner seated herself than he put his hand on her shoulder as he leaned in and placed a letter on the table before her. Instantly delicious heat flowed through her from his touch.

It was a letter from a local group. It referred to her recent visit and followed up her suggestion to seek royal approval for an initiative they'd discussed.

Eva tried to concentrate on the text. Yet she was too aware of Paul behind her, of the warm clasp of his hand and the soft feathering of his breath across her scalp.

It was only when he walked round to take his seat opposite her that she managed to fill her lungs properly.

Every time he touched her, there it was again. The need, almost overwhelming, to turn to him and give up pretending she didn't want him.

Memories of their night together interrupted her sleep. Sometimes, seeing Paul's face in repose, noting tired lines she hadn't registered before, she wondered if he suffered the same way. But he didn't push her to change her mind.

Eva told herself she should be thankful he'd taken her at her word. That he didn't try to pressure her.

Yet a carping voice inside declared it was because

he wasn't that attracted after all. One night had been enough for him.

How she detested that voice.

'You were a hit.'

Eva looked up, blinking into those mesmerising eyes, and took a moment to understand what he meant.

'Oh, the letter.' She lifted her shoulders. 'They were very enthusiastic. Very forward-thinking.'

'It sounds like you were too. Your suggestion was a good one. I'll have the relevant people look at it today.'

Eva glowed at his words, but made herself look away, reaching for a jug of fresh juice.

It was good to be appreciated but, she told herself, she couldn't allow herself to hang on Paul's approval as if it was the most important thing in her world. Soon she'd be moving on to an exciting new career surrounded by new people.

As soon as she worked out what that would be…

'Actually, if you're receptive to that, I had another idea I wanted to run past you.'

It was easier to talk about the needs of his people rather than her own need for him. These weeks sharing a new level of intimacy had only made her long for more.

Desperately she dragged her mind back to work, explaining the idea she'd had following a discussion with staff from an inner-city school.

'You want to give them access to the royal hunting lodge?' He leaned back in his seat, his brow pleating.

'Not the inside. Well…' She paused. 'That's another possibility but for the future.' She hurried on. 'These children live in a poor neighbourhood. They don't get out of the city, and here is a gorgeous, forested area close to the capital where they could—'

'Get lost and need a search-and-rescue team called in?'

Eva surveyed him steadily. This wasn't the response she'd expected. 'Is it really so dangerous there?'

Paul shrugged but she refused to be distracted into watching his powerful shoulders.

'If they venture up the mountain into the wildlife reserve.'

'But if it's a wildlife reserve, isn't there a boundary fence?'

'Well, yes, there is. A couple of kilometres from the lodge.'

'So a class group could visit the lodge, access the grounds but not go through into the reserve?'

Slowly Paul nodded but he didn't look enthusiastic. 'The place isn't set up for school groups. There aren't amenities for casual visitors.'

Eva sipped her juice then reached for some fresh figs and honey. 'I'm not suggesting letting a bunch of kids run wild and unsupervised in a heritage-listed building. My sources tell me there are amenities that can be unlocked at the back of the lodge—toilets and a basic kitchen that are quite separate to the rest of the building. They're in good condition but don't get used now there's no hunting there.'

'You *have* done your homework.' For once he didn't sound impressed. Eva tried to read his expression but couldn't.

'I thought you'd be pleased to put the place to good use. The smaller children would love it. Plus the older ones doing environmental studies or botany. And when I was talking to one of the art teachers it hit me how terrific the place would be for kids interested in sculpture. The plaster lobsters, for a start, would be fun inspiration.'

Eva waited for him to smile at that one but his mouth remained flat.

'You don't like the idea.'

She put down the honey and sat back, curiously deflated. It wasn't that she'd had an earth-shatteringly unique idea but that it had seemed a perfect use for a beautiful, neglected place.

The feeling of connection and partnership she'd begun to experience around Paul disintegrated under his frown.

'It's a very worthy proposal. I'll think about it. In the meantime—'

'*Why* don't you approve?'

Paul noted that obstinately raised chin and clear, questioning gaze and knew Eva wouldn't give up. It was her tenacious look.

He'd learned to respect it even if she chose the most inconvenient times to stand her ground. Such as these past weeks, sticking to her determination to avoid physical intimacy.

Maybe that was why he felt out of sorts. As if his skin didn't fit any more. After weeks living under the same roof, Paul was more than ever conscious of Eva sleeping a corridor away. Thirty metres and five doors away, to be precise.

More than once he'd prowled the distance in the middle of the night, drawn to her by a longing so fierce, so all-consuming, it drove him crazy.

But, instead of tapping on the door and waiting for her husky invitation, he'd stand there, hands clenching and unclenching, shoulders high and senses on alert for any sign that she was awake and waiting for him. Then he'd turn silently away and trudge back to his room, or more often his study or the gym, since sleep would elude him.

Because he respected her right to say no.

Even though he was going slowly out of his mind with frustration and thwarted longing.

'Paul?'

He blinked, focusing on bright eyes and parted lips. He recalled that moment when he leaned close, touching her shoulder, inhaling her fresh hyacinth scent, revelling in the fact she didn't shy away. But it wasn't nearly enough for a man raw with hunger.

'It's not a matter of approval. It's just—'

'You don't like it.'

The light had gone out of her bright eyes, snuffed out by his inability to share her enthusiasm.

'I'm considering it.'

She arched one eyebrow and waited, making him feel for the first time in years as if he had to explain himself.

Maybe he did. Eva knew a lot about his past but there was much he preferred to keep to himself. Territory he chose not to visit.

'On the face of it, it's an excellent idea.'

'But you're not happy about it. I thought you'd be pleased. The way you spoke about the lodge that night made it sound like you'd be happy to tear it down. I know it wouldn't create an income stream but at least this way someone would get benefit from the place.'

Paul reached for his coffee, sipping it slowly as he considered what, if anything, to tell her.

'You're right,' he said finally. 'Far better that it gets used.'

Eva said nothing, just regarded him across her untouched meal. She looked as if she'd happily sit there all morning if that was what it took.

Paul drained his cup and put it down with a decisive click.

'Look, it's just me being selfish, okay? But I promise the proposal will be considered properly.' In fact, it made so much sense he could just about guarantee the suggestion would become reality soon.

'You're not selfish.'

A huff of laughter escaped him. 'Of course I am. I'm just like anyone else.'

Eva shook her head, the morning light picking out strands of honey and caramel in her hair. 'You spend almost every waking hour working for your people, to help St Ancilla thrive. Your plan to release me from our engagement was for *my* benefit, and you're even promising to return my dowry, despite the fact it wasn't you who spent it. I've known you for years and have never seen you do a selfish thing yet.'

Paul stared at Eva, taken aback by her intensity as she leaned across the table.

'You make me sound…'

He shook his head. Didn't she realise what he'd done that night at the old lodge was pure selfishness? There'd been no noble holding back. One kiss was all it had taken for his vaunted control to drop, and he'd grabbed for what he wanted.

'I'm no knight in shining armour, Eva. The simple fact is I think of the old lodge as my private place, and now I discover I don't like sharing.'

'I wondered if it might be something like that,' she surprised him by saying. 'You love it there so much?'

Love? The place had been a punishment then later a bolthole.

'My attachment to the place is complicated.'

Eva folded her hands together on the table as if waiting for him to continue.

Paul gave a mental shrug. Why not?

He sat back in his chair. 'My father was…' *Appalling. Irascible. Impossible to please.* 'Difficult. Very difficult. Everything had to be done his way. He tried to mould me into a copy of himself.'

'I'm so glad he didn't succeed.'

Paul felt a little jab of heat through the chest at Eva's words. It was true he'd made it his life's aim *not* to be like King Hugo, but hearing Eva say so, especially when she smiled at him that way…

'My mother ran interference when she could but, from the time I was old enough to realise what sort of man my father really was, we were on a collision course. Nothing I did was good enough. I wasn't hard enough, didn't follow his instructions blindly. As a result, I was punished regularly.'

Eva's expression grew tight with disapproval. 'He beat you?'

What would have happened if Paul's mother had

turned such a look on her husband when he'd lost his temper instead of turning meekly away?

He shrugged. 'Yes. But eventually only rarely, because it didn't have the desired effect.' Because Paul had been too proud and too determined to let the old man see how close he was to breaking.

'He tried other methods. One day, when I'd questioned something he said, he had me packed off to the hunting lodge. Told me that if I wanted to be so bloody independent I could have a taste of real independence and see how I fared. I assume he thought I'd give up after a day and ask to come back with my tail between my legs. Or that it would be a salutary, toughening up experience.'

'I don't understand. Why would staying at the lodge be tough?'

Paul felt a grim smile tug at his lips. 'Because I was only nine. I was left there alone in the middle of winter. The electricity was turned off and the water. I was given a couple of days' rations but no matches. The guards posted at the perimeter had orders not to let me out till I said I was ready to apologise.'

Across the table, Eva's jaw dropped open. 'That's… that's…'

'That was my father.' Paul reached out for a pastry and bit into it with relish. Even now he recalled how sharp true hunger pangs were, and how harsh even a Mediterranean winter could be.

'After five days, the captain of the guard was allowed in to see how I was doing.'

'Five days!' She shot to her feet, her hands planted

on the table. 'He left a nine-year-old alone there for five days? What sort of parent...?'

She choked down the rest of the sentence, making Paul feel all sorts of a fool for distressing her.

Seconds later he was on her side of the table, taking hold of her hands. Her fingers felt cold as they clutched his.

'Shh. It's okay. I survived.'

'But that's just *criminal*!'

'That was my father. You're not supposed to say it about a parent, but it's a relief he's dead. He can't harm us any more. Plus, we're spared the need to put him on trial for his crimes against the state.'

Still Eva goggled up at him. 'But *five days*! How did you survive?'

'Well, I was skinnier when they took me home than when I went there.'

Instantly Paul regretted his wry words as he saw her horror.

'It wasn't too bad, really, even though my attempts to trap animals to eat were a dismal failure. I had more success with heating, though, so I was warm. I'd seen a documentary showing people lighting fires by rubbing sticks together. It took me a day and a half—' and hands rubbed raw to the point of bleeding '—but I finally managed it. I set water traps outside to collect rainfall so I had enough to drink. It was actually a bit of an adventure, camping out in one of the smaller rooms with a stack of books from the library and a roaring fire.'

Compared with his regimented life at the palace, it had been bliss. Except for the hunger pains, and those times in the middle of the night when his nine-year-old imagination had turned the lodge into a terrifying place.

'He was a monster.' Eva clutched Paul's hands and his fingers curled around hers.

Even Paul's mother, though supposedly worn out with worry about him all those years ago, had welcomed him home by trying to make him promise never to cross his father again. It felt good now, having someone so unequivocally on his side, even after all this time.

But it was more than that. This wasn't just anyone, this was *Eva*. The fact that she cared so much, even about ancient wrongs like that, made him feel something he'd never felt before.

He felt fuller, as if emotions rose so close to the surface they scraped at his skin. Yet he felt stronger too, as if her caring ignited a fire in him he hadn't known about.

'He's gone now.' He wanted to wrap his arms around Eva and pull her close. It seemed the most natural thing in the world. To comfort her, and himself. To be together.

Paul stiffened his spine and fought the impulse, trying to respect the boundaries she'd set. Instead he lifted one of those cool hands to his lips and kissed her knuckles.

'It's not so bad, Eva. After that my father realised how futile it was trying to discipline me that way. Instead he'd simply banish me for a week or so till he could stand seeing me again.'

'Not to the hunting lodge!'

He smiled against her hand. 'It was never mentioned, but after that there was always power and water and plenty of food. I developed a love-hate relationship with the place but, even after all these years, if ever I need time and space I head off to the lodge, which is why there were sheets on the bed and provisions in the kitchen.'

He lowered her hand but kept hold of it. 'From a purely financial point of view, the old place doesn't pay its way. Though in the last couple of years it's been used for staff retreats and planning sessions. Principally, though, it's my bolthole.'

'Then you should have said so upfront. It doesn't *have* to be opened to school groups.'

Paul shook his head. 'Why shouldn't they get some benefit from it? You're right. It's in an amazing setting and it's selfish not to share.'

'I never said you were...'

This time he couldn't resist the lure of that quaint little frown and her pouting lips. He swooped down for a brief kiss, luxuriating in the taste and softness of that lovely mouth before pulling back.

Satisfaction filled him as he saw her dazed eyes and their hint of smoky blue.

In that moment Paul came to a decision. Not with logic or argument but with pure instinct. And nothing had ever felt so right.

Eva was his.

It didn't matter if their betrothal had been arranged as an affair of state, or that the reason they were still officially engaged was to preserve her reputation and scotch any scandal.

Eva was his and he wanted it to stay that way. He

wanted her. Wanted her in his bed, but wanted much more besides.

Eva was his and he intended to claim her as his bride.

The thought of her as his wife, not merely his fiancée, brought on that burgeoning emotion, filling up all the empty cracks and fissures he hadn't known *were* empty till these last few weeks, when he'd begun to yearn for more.

On impulse, he raised both her hands to his lips, drawing in the delicate, sweet scent of her skin, watching her eyes widen and her mouth soften.

He was a determined man.

He was determined to keep Eva. All he had to do was find out how.

CHAPTER ELEVEN

A WEEK LATER, Paul invited Eva back to his study after an official reception.

Usually he hosted such events alone. Tonight, with Eva circulating among the foreign delegates and charming them, Paul had felt some of his burden lift. It had been an important event, designed to encourage interest in doing business here in St Ancilla. And, from the discussions he'd had, the signs were encouraging.

As he led her along the corridor it struck him that Eva had been lightening his load for several weeks. She allowed him more time to pursue the discussions he needed to while she acted the perfect hostess.

More, she often gave him a valuable different perspective, noticing things he hadn't. Details that helped him at the negotiating table. But other things too, such as reminding him his work shouldn't be all about securing the nation's finances. More than once she'd brought his focus back to small-scale local issues that made such a difference to his people.

Like school excursions for disadvantaged students. He remembered her delight when she'd heard that the first such outing to the hunting lodge had been a success. And the way her eyes had shone when he'd announced the purchase of a bus to be shared by several city schools for excursions.

After years of public austerity, the finances weren't quite so tight, and it felt good to direct funds where they'd benefit the people.

'Here we are.' He opened the door and stood aside for Eva to enter.

He caught her spring scent as she moved past him, elegant and desirable in a gown that looked as if it was made of dusky-pink cobwebs, ethereal and enticing. Another dress by a local designer. In a few short weeks Eva was putting St Ancillan fashion on the international map.

Right now, though, Paul was more interested in imagining his hands around that slim waist, or slipping up under the delicate skirt to touch silky skin.

'Paul…?'

'Sorry.' He dragged his gaze to her face, noting a hint of fatigue around her eyes. He ushered her to a seat but she shook her head.

'I'm tired so I won't stay long.'

Disappointment stirred. They had developed a habit of retiring here or to his private sitting room to unwind and discuss the day. Another luxury he'd only just discovered and had no intention of giving up.

'I won't keep you long. Have I been working you too hard?'

Something, some hint of emotion, rippled across Eva's features but was gone so fast he might have imagined it.

Except Paul noticed everything about her now. He

was reminded of the early days of their engagement, when she'd hide her emotions behind a polite façade.

His gut squeezed at the idea of Eva retreating from him. He wanted to find out why she was so fatigued and fix it. Except her very posture, perfectly poised and regal, spoke volumes to a man who knew her. He guessed sheer willpower kept her upright after a long evening of formal entertaining.

Quickly he turned to his desk, unlocking a deep drawer and withdrawing a crimson velvet box that had been brought up from the treasury.

He moved to where she stood, the box unaccountably heavy in his hand. This was a threshold he was about to cross, yet he had no qualms about it. Giving this to Eva made sense in every possible way. But he felt the gravity of the moment. Felt and welcomed it.

'I'd like you to wear this at the ball next week.'

His birthday ball. What better time to share his intentions with Eva? He'd been tempted to tell her tonight but it wasn't the right time. He preferred not to blurt it out when she was longing for her bed. He wanted her full attention. The moment had to be perfect.

Hesitantly she took the box, her forehead crinkling in curiosity. Then she snapped open the lid and any sign of weariness was banished by surprise. Her face lit with the reflection of light bouncing off the gems she held.

'I don't think—'

'Wear it for me, Eva. Please.' Paul couldn't remember ever hanging on a woman's answer quite so urgently.

He reminded himself it was just a tiara. That the important thing would be winning Eva's agreement to stay with him. But within the St Ancillan royal family this piece held great significance. It was proof of his intentions at a time when he still trod warily around Eva's doubts and fears.

He'd taken advantage of her once, making love to her when she'd been vulnerable, and it could be argued she wasn't thinking straight. This, for the sake of his own conscience, was his promise to her, even if she didn't know that yet.

'Are you sure? It's absolutely gorgeous, of course, but—'

'It's the most formal occasion on the royal calendar. If you'd known you'd be here for it, you'd have brought something similar from Tarentia, wouldn't you?'

'Yes, I would have.' Her eyes lifted from the brilliant stones to his face and Paul felt that for once he'd managed to counter her objections easily.

'You'll look stunning wearing it.' He didn't dare reach out and touch her, knowing the temptation to do more than allow a fleeting caress would be too strong. 'You'd look stunning without it, I know, but it might have been made especially for you. I'd be honoured if you'd wear it. For me, Eva.'

For a second something bright and potent shimmered between them. Later he'd wonder if it was the radiance of light sparking off aquamarines and diamonds, but in this moment Paul knew, *felt*, it was more. A moment's communion between them. An instant of shared emotion.

His heart lifted as Eva closed the box and nodded. 'Thank you, Paul. I will.'

Eva crossed her room on wobbly legs that gave way when she reached the wide bed. Her fingers bit into the crimson velvet of the box as she subsided onto the mattress.

Her thoughts were a whirling mess that matched a stomach unsettled by nerves. All day she'd been on edge, worried but telling herself not to be.

It had been difficult to concentrate on her role as hostess as a voice of doubt kept nagging at her.

Then, just as she'd thought she could escape to the solitude of her suite, Paul had waylaid her. She should have forestalled him, pleaded tiredness straight away, but she'd been either too light-headed to think of it or too weak to resist the temptation of a little time alone with him.

She feared it was the latter. Though she knew it was bad for her, that this need for his company was something she had to wean herself off. The desire to make the most of their last weeks together was too strong.

Slowly she unlatched the lid of the antique box and lifted it. Instantly the room seemed brighter. It was a classically elegant piece, a master jeweller's work from over a century ago.

Fashioned from platinum, it was set with stones of graduating size, the largest at the front angling down to smaller, yet still magnificent emerald-cut stones on either side. The gems were aquamarines, a pure, clear pale blue, set in a delicate frame of looping diamonds that sparkled brilliantly.

Even she, brought up seeing and wearing heirloom gems regularly, had rarely seen a piece so exquisite.

And Paul thinks it could have been made especially for me.

Her heart pounded an out-of-kilter beat and something behind her ribs caught.

He's exaggerating.

But part of her wanted to believe it was true. That he found her attractive. That he believed she shone as brightly as these amazing stones.

Had he known she'd be wearing silver next week? That this would be the perfect match to the gown being designed for her?

No, it was a lucky chance. That was all.

Yet part of her, a tiny superstitious part she didn't know, felt she was *fated* to wear this.

As if!

Reluctantly she closed the lid, cutting off the blinding brilliance, groping for sanity, perspective.

He just wants you to look good at his birthday ball. It's nothing personal.

But it had felt personal. Sounded it.

In her head Eva replayed his voice, deeper than usual and carving a groove of longing through her stupid heart, asking her to wear it *for him.*

The way he'd looked at her.

Even through her stress and tiredness, she'd seen that look and felt herself tremble in anticipation.

Or was she reading too much into a glance and a simple act of kindness? He was lending her a tiara so she'd look the part of his fiancée at a significant event.

One she hadn't originally been invited to because he'd planned to end their engagement.

That severed her wayward imaginings.

Paul was making the best of a difficult situation.

He had no idea how much more difficult her continued presence was making things. Only today, at a visit to an embroiderers' guild, she'd been asked if they might have the honour of working on her wedding dress.

Within the last two weeks she'd fielded similar requests from lace makers and from the designer responsible for tonight's fabulous dress.

Each time she was asked, Eva felt sicker in the stomach. Because she was living a lie and now others were investing in it, building their hopes on it. Eagerly awaiting the wedding.

She'd been stunned by the alacrity with which most St Ancillans had welcomed her. There'd been a few who'd looked askance, as if doubting her suitability as a consort for their King. And still there'd been a few sensational articles about her, works of total fiction. But she didn't let those bother her.

No, what bothered her was the feeling that she was sinking deeper and deeper into this mire of make-believe. That with every passing day it would be harder to break free.

Because she wanted to be what everyone believed her to be—Paul's intended bride.

And then there was the other worry. The one that had haunted her since last night when she'd realised she'd been in St Ancilla a whole month.

The possibility, faint but disturbing, that she might be pregnant.

CHAPTER TWELVE

IT WAS LATE and Eva had already danced with a who's who of dignitaries. She'd chatted with ambassadors and made small talk with a host of St Ancillans, some of whom were familiar to her now. There was an air of jubilation and good will, as if this celebration signalled more than Paul's birthday. As if people knew that, after years of austerity, things were looking up.

Eva enjoyed herself, especially the two waltzes with Paul, clasped close in his embrace as if he'd never heard of royal protocol and simply wanted to envelop her. Her heart still hammered too fast after the sheer delight of swirling through the glittering crowd, lost to the joy of being in his arms.

But reality had intervened soon enough. It had been in the supper room, when she'd been confronted with a plate of tiny pancakes topped with smoked salmon and gleaming caviar.

She'd tried to tell herself it was the heat and the press of the crowd, but for a moment she'd felt nausea well. Instantly she'd retreated, excusing herself for the quiet of a withdrawing room, taking slow breaths and dampening her nape and wrists with cold water.

She was fine now. No more nausea. It was probably just nerves.

Except she'd been in St Ancilla five weeks and still hadn't had her period.

Usually that wouldn't bother her. Eva's cycle was notoriously irregular. Which meant she was worrying about nothing.

Except this time there was just a possibility she was pregnant. Condoms weren't a hundred percent effective.

Heat danced in her veins as she remembered Paul straining against her. His hoarse shout of elation as he'd powered into her and she'd been swept up into bliss.

Yes, pregnancy was definitely a possibility.

But not, she told herself, probable. And the more she fretted...who knew? Could stress delay her period?

She needed to take a pregnancy test.

She wasn't able to leave the palace, walk into a pharmacy and ask for a test kit. The world would know within hours.

Instead she'd contacted her best friend and asked her to buy one and send it to her. A courier had arrived with the parcel while Eva had been dressing for the ball. She'd been torn between the need to discover the truth straight away and the knowledge that she'd never maintain the façade of calm she needed at the royal event if she discovered she was pregnant.

Or if she discovered she wasn't. Eva was honest enough to realise part of her would be disappointed at the news she wasn't carrying Paul's child, despite the complications a baby would create.

Tonight, as soon as she returned to her suite, she'd take the test.

Decision made, she stood straighter before the mirror, taking time to smooth a stray lock of hair, fixing it back into the low-set knot behind her head. She smoothed the glittering silver dress with hands that barely trembled. On her head sat the gorgeous tiara Paul had loaned her.

Wearing this dress and jewellery, she looked the part of Paul's bride-to-be. All she had to do was keep her composure a little longer and she could escape to her room.

Eva hadn't counted on the pair of women gossiping at a side entrance to the ballroom.

They stood with their backs to her, yet their voices carried down the otherwise deserted corridor.

'Do you think it's true, that she really was trawling night clubs looking for a one-night stand? That she's the sort who's never satisfied with just one man?'

'It's possible. That photo…' A shrug of plump shoulders. 'On the other hand, you noticed what she's wearing, of course.'

'It's an amazing gown. I'll give her that. She dresses well.'

'Not the dress, the tiara. My sister-in-law used to be a lady-in-waiting to the old Queen. If I remember rightly, that's the tiara she told me about. The one that's never been worn by anyone but the Queen of Ancilla. Now, I ask you, would he give her that to wear if he knew she was some little tart he can't trust to keep her legs together?'

Eva faltered to a stop, stunned. Not by the carelessly vicious gossip but by the news she was apparently wearing something that rightly belonged to the country's Queen.

Could it be true? Why would Paul let her wear it in that case? They were due to end their engagement soon. Such a gesture could only dredge up more speculation about them.

Her heart thundered and her skin prickled all over as she tried to make sense of the gesture. But this wasn't the time or the place. Any minute now, the gossips would turn and see her.

Too late. Her half-formed thought of heading back the way she'd come died as the women both sank into deep curtseys.

There, stepping out of the ballroom in front of them, was Paul, the scowl on his face as black as his superbly tailored evening clothes.

Eva sucked in a deep breath, stunned by the cold fury on his face. She'd seen him look like that only once before, when discussing the man who'd taken advantage of her behind the night club. Then he'd looked as though he'd wanted to commit murder.

Now she watched his features settle into a mask of glacial calm. He spoke to the women, but so low she didn't catch his words. An instant later they were hurrying away, heads down, as if glad to escape.

As they left his eyes caught hers. Heat stole through her and a jangle of emotions stirred. Eva set her shoulders and moved towards him, head up.

'Eva. I...' He paused as someone spoke to him from inside the ballroom. Then he held out his hand to her. 'Come. It's time for our final dance.'

'Then we need to talk.'

He nodded, holding her eyes. 'We do, indeed. We have something important to discuss.'

The rest of the ball alternately flew and dragged by.

Dancing another waltz in Paul's arms was a brief, glorious respite from doubt and anxiety. Even the fact that he held her closer than ever, his body moving in sync with hers so deftly they might have been one, was a source of joy rather than dismay. But then came the long, ceremonial process of farewelling their guests.

Eva didn't see the two women who'd been talking outside the ballroom. Had they left without saying good-bye, or had Paul ordered them gone?

Whatever the truth, by the time they settled upstairs in Paul's private sitting room Eva was exhausted and nervous. Both of which she refused to show.

When Paul offered her a drink, she asked for sparkling water. A whisky was tempting—she'd appreciate that sudden shot of heat, as she felt unaccountably chilled—but until she knew there was no pregnancy she'd avoid alcohol.

She sat stiff-backed on a sofa, while he sprawled, long-legged on one facing her.

They both began speaking at once then stopped. Paul gestured for her to go first.

'Is it true?' she asked in a voice brittle with suppressed emotion. 'What that woman said about this tiara?'

'You understood that? They were speaking Ancillan. I thought you weren't fluent.'

Eva pursed her lips. 'We've been engaged for four years, Paul. Of course I've been learning your language.' In fact, she'd started many years earlier, even though it was a notoriously difficult language to learn, because of her infatuation with Paul.

If only it were still just infatuation!

For the first time she could recall, he looked flustered. 'I knew you'd had lessons. I've heard you speak a little at official events. But I thought…' His gaze sharpened. 'Did you understand what your attacker said in that back alley?'

Eva sipped her water and inclined her head, suppressing a shiver. Occasionally she still heard that voice, those words, in her dreams.

'Eva!' He leaned forward, as if to reach for her, and she sank back, feeling too fragile to let him touch her.

Paul frowned. 'In that case, allow me to apologise on behalf of my fellow Ancillans. I wouldn't have had you hear such things for anything, either that night or tonight. Those harpies—'

'Was it true? About the tiara?'

He swirled amber liquid around his glass.

'The piece is from the family vault. It's been worn by several generations of women in my family.' His sudden smile was like sunshine breaking through a stormy sky. 'It could have been made for you, Eva. I'm so pleased you wore it.'

With difficulty Eva ignored the compliment and concentrated on what he'd said about the tiara. She'd guessed it was a special piece, given its obvious age and quality.

'She said it was only ever worn by the Queen. Is that right?'

Paul hesitated before answering then shrugged. 'Traditionally, yes.'

'And this is generally known?' Her skin frosted as she absorbed the implications of what she'd done, wearing the beautiful thing. 'Does everyone see this as proof we'll marry soon?'

Already she found it increasingly difficult, fending off well-meant queries about when the wedding would be. After their long engagement, it seemed people believed it was imminent. Paul hadn't thought of that when he'd suggested she stay here for six weeks.

His dark eyebrows crammed together as if he didn't like her words. 'Very few people would understand the significance of you wearing it.'

'But some in the court clearly do. They see it as further proof that we're to marry.' Eva paused, throat closing on the word. This act of theirs grew harder each day.

He put down his glass and shot to the edge of his seat, leaning forward and capturing her free hand.

'Does it matter what others think?'

'It does if they expect a wedding in a few months. Hasn't it struck you that we're digging ourselves into an ever deeper hole by continuing this pretend engagement? That we're building up public expectations?'

Something shifted in Paul's expression.

'What if it's not a pretence? What if I said I wanted you to stay and marry me?'

Her restless fingers froze in his grip. 'Sorry?'

'What if I asked you to wear the tiara because I want you to be my Queen?'

'You're not serious?'

But, looking into those dark blue eyes, she saw no hint of humour, much less doubt. Paul looked like a man convinced he knew what he was doing.

A great wave of emotion shuddered through her and she had the simultaneous desire to laugh and burst into tears.

Shock, she realised. She was in shock.

Eva lifted her glass to trembling lips and downed her water in one draught. She gripped the tumbler so hard it felt as though it were soldered to her skin.

'What are you saying, Paul?'

'I'm saying we're good together, Eva.'

'Just because we were sexually compatible.' He'd never know how much it cost her to use the past tense. She still burned for him. Just having him hold her hand incinerated her control and left her longing to be possessed by him.

His mouth quirked up on one side and inevitably there it was. Desire, like hot honey, swirling through her.

'Actually, I wasn't referring to sex. I've been trying very, very hard not to think about that, though I admit I haven't been very successful.'

He paused, watching her face intently as his thumb swiped across her wrist, as if he knew that made her shaky with longing. 'But, yes, you're right. We're extremely compatible physically. I'd even say combustible. I can't stop thinking about us, together.'

Another pause in which Eva would swear she saw a heat haze shimmer in the air between them.

'We share something very special sexually.'

That rough-suede voice was a caress. Eva's nipples peaked as her skin drew taut and everything inside clenched.

'That night was a mistake.'

'It was no mistake, Eva. But let's put that aside for now.'

Easier said than done when she felt as if she was on fire just from his words.

'We're good together. We understand each other. We have similar values and goals. We make a great team— you must see that.'

Eva clamped her lips shut, scared of what she might blurt out.

'These last few weeks have been a revelation. I never realised how much difference it would make to have a partner beside me.' He shook his head. 'Even in such a short time you've made a difference here and you've lessened my load. I actually feel like I don't have to work sixteen hours a day just to keep the place afloat.'

Inside something seemed to unfurl. Like petals of a flower opening.

Eva was glad she'd made a difference. It was what she'd trained for, after all, but mainly she'd wanted to help Paul. She'd found a real sense of achievement in the weeks since she'd been here. Imagine what she'd be able to do with more time.

A hint of a smile hovered at the corners of her mouth. She felt the quiver, felt the rising joy, for just an instant before she suppressed it.

Paul's voice was deep and serious. 'Our arrangement has been working so well. Why not make it permanent?'

His eyes glowed and his expression was almost tender.

Almost.

Because sexual desire and an appreciation of her work ethic and skills wasn't love. It might make her feel good but it wasn't enough.

Eva had changed since she'd arrived in St Ancilla. Perhaps she saw more clearly how futile it was to hope for more than Paul could give. Perhaps she'd set a higher value on herself and wasn't ready to settle for less than she needed.

Paul saw the benefits of an arranged marriage. The convenience. That was all. He didn't see *her*. Or, if he did, only in so far as she filled his own needs.

He wasn't a selfish man. He didn't know how she felt about him. If he did, she guessed he'd never suggest marriage. But her feelings were already shredded from playing the part of his fiancée up close and personal this last month. Imagine how tough it would be if they married!

'I'm glad to be able to help, Paul.' His name felt heavy on her lips.

She breathed slowly and put her empty glass down on a side table. Then she gently tugged her other hand free of his grip.

A second later she was on her feet.

She had to end this. Now.

And, if you're pregnant, then what?

But she couldn't be, surely? How unlikely was it that there was a baby? He'd taken precautions, hadn't he?

She pressed a hand to her stomach then let it fall, scared he might read the tell-tale gesture.

If there's a baby, then we'll just have to face that complication when the time comes.

For now, all she could do was face her current reality.

That Paul wanted her in a convenient marriage. He'd be a kind, caring husband but he would never love her.

While she was still, despite her every effort, head over heels in love with him.

Eva paced towards the window, peering out at moonlight silvering the Mediterranean. It looked so lovely, so perfectly romantic. But this wasn't a romance, it was reality.

'It wouldn't work, Paul. I don't want to marry you.' She kept her eyes fixed on the view, knowing she wouldn't be able to do this if she looked him in the eye.

'In fact, the reason I wanted to talk with you tonight was to tell you I've decided to go home next week.'

'Next week!' His voice came from behind her and she felt the warmth of his breath cascade down her bare neck, sending tiny ripples of delight skittering across her skin. He must be standing close, his head tilted down towards her. For a second she allowed herself to imagine that was regret as well as surprise in his voice. 'But you can't. It's not—'

'It's what's going to happen, Paul. I can't do this any more.'

Eva swung round and was confronted with the sight of his solid jaw clenched tight. She knew Paul, knew how determined he could be. She couldn't afford to give him a chance to win her over because she knew how fragile her defences were against him.

'Please, Paul. No more arguments. We've been over this before. I don't want to marry you, and you don't want to marry an unwilling woman.'

Was it her imagination, or did he flinch?

Eva couldn't stay to find out. Without raising her gaze to his, lest she waver, she hurried past him. Out she went into the cold, empty corridor, her bruised heart lying heavy against her ribs.

He didn't try to stop her.

That hurt most of all.

CHAPTER THIRTEEN

Paul paced the corridor. The place was in darkness but for pearly moonlight spilling through the windows. The clean-up from the ball had finished and everyone was in bed.

Except him.

Eva's announcement had come out of the blue, her news so shocking it was impossible to relax and switch off. He kept reliving her words and that terrible air of finality as she'd spoken. It hadn't been posturing. She'd meant every word.

Why?

He couldn't understand it. Her attitude made no sense.

Her words had sliced through him, as if she'd taken one of the antique swords from a display case downstairs and run him through with it.

Had he ever known such hurt? It made the time he'd fractured his collarbone on the polo field fade into insignificance. Even discovering the full extent of his father's crimes against the nation and against his half-sister Caro hadn't hurt like this. Because he'd been able to do something to correct those.

But Eva leaving—not just for a couple of months but for ever—there was no remedy for that.

Paul's pain increased, as if that phantom blade cut down through his chest and kept going. He stopped mid-stride, pressing his palm to his belly, trying to force the sensation away.

He hadn't seen this coming. He'd imagined Eva was happy here. She seemed it. Her enthusiasm for the projects she was engaged in and the people she met brightened each day. The only negative was that she was on edge whenever he got close. Then he'd see her shoulders creep up as if she was girding herself for his touch.

But he understood that too—sexual frustration. Because whenever he touched her there were sparks. They'd start at the point of contact and spread right through him. And he'd swear she felt those sparks too. He'd caught Eva's dazed look as he'd wrapped his hand around her waist to waltz, or held her close beside him while they'd entertained guests. Soon, he promised himself, she'd be his again. Because the physical connection between them was impossible to ignore.

He'd assumed she must be as frustrated as he at her 'no sex' rule, yet he'd held back, respecting her need for time and space. Even if…

Paul's thoughts frayed as he noticed something down the corridor. A line of light under Eva's door. It was close to three a.m. and she was still up.

He didn't hesitate. He'd been trained to take charge, to make things happen.

In two beats of his heart he was at her door, head inclined, listening. Was that movement inside?

He raised his hand and tapped on the solid wood.

For several seconds he waited, listening, then tapped again. He was reaching for the handle when the door swung open.

Golden lamplight silhouetted her, congealing his thoughts into a hard knot in his gut. Eva's hair was loose on her shoulders and she'd wrapped a robe around herself, cinched tight at her waist.

Paul's breath dried out, like a mistral wind sighing out of his lungs in an arid rush.

She was beautiful.

But she was more than simply beautiful.

He didn't have the words to do her justice. There was just the heavy thrum of his heart beating *mine, mine, mine*.

'It's very late, Paul. I need to...'

Paul inserted a shoulder in the gap between door and jamb and kept moving. The gap widened. For a second they stood toe to toe, so close her heat drenched him, then she moved back and he shut the door behind them.

Eva rubbed her arms as if she were cold, her hands disappearing up the wide sleeves of her robe. It was pale silk, with a delicate pattern of wisteria blossom, making him think, as her long straight hair swung across it, of geishas and oriental luxury.

The notion intensified when she moved, her breasts shifting free against the thin material, and he realised she was naked beneath the patterned silk.

He'd been going to say something but now the words eluded him. He swallowed hard as he took her in.

She spoke but for a couple of seconds it was lost in the white noise of his blood pumping hard, roaring in his ears.

Eva folded her arms in an attitude of annoyance, pulling the fabric tight over her breasts, and dimly he realised she was waiting for him to answer whatever she'd said. Paul dragged his gaze back to her up-thrust chin and prim mouth.

'You're angry.'

'I'm tired, Paul. There's no point rehashing our last discussion. I want to go to sleep.'

With a clarity that tasted bitter in his mouth, he noticed she wasn't talking about rehashing the discussion *tonight*. She meant *ever*. She'd had her say and didn't want to open the subject again.

'Yet you're still awake. What's the trouble? Too much on your mind to sleep?'

He glanced over her shoulder and noticed a suitcase open on an antique carved trunk. It was half-full.

Ice shafted through him, chilling his blood.

She was packing?

Didn't she mean to wait till next week, as she'd said?

Urgency gripped him, twisting his gut into knots.

He'd planned to talk to her tomorrow. Convince her to stay. He could be persuasive, and he'd had no doubts he could make Eva change her mind—or at least agree to stay a little longer, which would give him the time he needed to…what?

It was obvious she'd already thought things through. That, all the time he'd imagined her enjoying herself, she'd been counting the days till she left.

And yet there were times, lots of them, when he'd sensed she was anything but distant or uninterested.

'I often don't sleep straight away after an event late in the evening. But I was just about to turn the light off.' Her gaze flickered away from his and he knew she was lying.

To make him go.

Because she didn't want to give him the chance to change her mind?

Because she intended to leave sooner than she'd said?

It seemed only too likely.

She wouldn't listen to him. Wouldn't be persuaded.

But there was one way he might get through to her.

Paul wasn't even conscious of forming the thought when he found his fingers brushing the softness of her cheek, down past her chin to her throat then feathering up to push into the heavy curtain of her hair.

Her breath was a sharp inhale and her eyes widened, catching his. She opened her mouth, probably to stop him, so he raked his fingers purposefully across her scalp, moulding her skull as he lowered his head.

Eva's words never came.

He felt the puff of warm air from her mouth to his, scant centimetres away, but there was no objection.

Her head seemed heavier in his grip, as if she tilted back into his touch, leaving her face turned up towards his. Even then Paul waited, watching, breathing her in, till he saw, like a mist parting over the sea, a hint of blue in the steamy grey of her eyes.

Something stabbed at his chest. Not pain this time. Satisfaction. Anticipation. Relief.

He breathed deeper, inhaling her sweet floral and woman scent, feeling it go straight to his head.

'I want you, Eva. So badly. And I think you want me.' He slid his other hand around her waist, drawing her flush against him before she could conjure words to push him away.

Paul watched those expressive eyes, expecting rejection, waiting for the flash of sudden anger.

It didn't come. Instead there was her scent curling around him, her warm body lush and soft, and those eyes, those incredible eyes, wide with... Yearning? Invitation?

He didn't need more. His mouth touched hers and paused, waiting, till her lips trembled and opened. Slim hands grasped his shoulders, fingers tightening, and he swept her up against him, delving deep into her mouth with a hungry, desperate kiss.

It wasn't suave or practised. This kiss was too full of urgency and a relief that teetered on the brink of fear that any second now she'd push him away.

Teeth rubbed, lips and noses squashed, but it didn't matter. Because the desperation wasn't just his, it was hers too. He felt it in the clutch of her hands and the arch of her body.

'Eva...' he breathed against her mouth, tilting her head back with his hand so he could pepper her face then her throat with urgent kisses. 'I need you, darling. I can't...'

He couldn't say it. *I can't let you go.*

Instead he showed her with his mouth, his hands, his body pressing against hers, how much he needed her.

Her hands were in his hair, fingers tunnelling across his scalp, dragging his head lower as if she feared he might try to escape.

Paul worked his way back up to her mouth and kissed

her hard, tongue tangling with hers, and still he couldn't get enough of her.

He needed more. So much more.

Wrapping both arms around Eva, he hoisted her off the ground, still kissing her. With eyes barely slitted open, he covered the space between door and bed. The back of her legs hit the mattress and they tumbled down.

Eva's robe came unfastened in the manoeuvre and he slipped one hand past woven silk to skin just as soft and luxurious. His fingers spread wide, covering her hip then sliding across her abdomen.

'Paul.' It was a husk of sound. So raw and soft he couldn't tell if it was entreaty or protest. Reluctantly he opened his eyes and lifted his head.

Her gaze captured his, misty blue and approving. Her hands moved down from his shoulders and tugged at his shirt, dragging it open regardless of buttons.

Triumph stirred. And something more profound. His chest welled with it, his arteries fizzed and his mouth curved up into a smile that dragged already taut flesh even tighter.

He cleared his throat, intending to tell her how much she meant to him. But she leaned in and bit him on the side of the neck, right at the most sensitive spot, then suckled there, soothing the pinprick of hurt with a lavish wave of erotic delight.

Paul's heart hammered so fast it seemed to tumble in his chest. Especially when she pushed him a little to one side, enough to tug at his belt.

He'd been intending to take this slow, to seduce her by slow degrees till there was no possibility she'd consider—ever—the idea of leaving him. His intentions disintegrated at the feel of her fumbling at his waist. Instead he reached into his back pocket and withdrew the condom he'd got into the habit of carrying these last weeks—in case the opportunity to use it arrived.

This time, despite Eva's questing hands, he managed to ditch his shoes, socks, underwear and trousers, though his shirt still hung open off his shoulders as he settled between her bare thighs.

The blurring urgency of the last few moments stilled as they lay together, Eva's robe wide open so he could feast his eyes on her bare breasts bobbing high with each shallow breath. But, delightful as the sight was, Paul's attention kept going back to her blue-grey eyes. The warmth and emotion he saw there.

This was more than a carnal coupling. Eva's expression told a story that felt familiar. Surely it matched what he felt?

That moment of wondering, of profound feeling, seemed to last for ever. But Paul was only human and now Eva's hands moved again, her legs sliding further open, so he sank lower between her hips.

'Eva, I—'

'Paul, please...'

Propped above her, he lifted his hand to her face and brushed a strand of hair back. He trailed his fingers down her brow and her cheek, undone by the welling tenderness he felt for this woman.

Who moved first, he didn't know, but that first slight shift shattered the stillness. They came together easily, every tilt of the body, every caress of hands and lips, stoking an incredible intensity of feeling. As if in slow motion, Paul registered each exquisite sensation, even as their rhythm quickened. Till, finally, it was too much. Taking this slowly wasn't possible when every touch felt so good. *They* felt so good together.

Eva's fingers dug into his shoulders and she arched against him in a move that tore the last of his control and left him hovering on the brink.

He heard his name shouted in ecstasy, and then she was bucking against him, dragging him over the precipice with her into piercing, perfect bliss.

A long time later, with Eva dozing at his shoulder, Paul decided he had to move. He needed to dispose of the condom. The difficulty was that his bones felt like overcooked noodles and he wasn't sure he could stand.

Moving slowly, so as not to wake her, he slid from the bed and rose, taking a moment to adjust to the world again. He felt sated, exhausted, and yet his blood fizzed with elation. It felt like a weight had crumbled from his shoulders.

A smile tugged at his mouth as he entered the bathroom.

Eva and he still had to talk, obviously, but at least there'd be no more pretence that she didn't want him. Whatever was holding Eva back, they'd work it out together.

He was washing his hands when he caught sight of a box at the far end of the marble counter.

Paul blinked. He had twenty-twenty vision and didn't need to move closer to read the writing on it. But he did, drawn by a force that knocked any lingering satisfaction from his mind.

A pregnancy-test kit.

Everything inside him stilled, then his heart began to gallop.

Was Eva pregnant?

Was that why she was so determined to leave?

But that would mean…

Paul told himself it couldn't be true.

Yet, surely this was evidence?

She'd tested herself for pregnancy and announced she was leaving, despite the incredible chemistry they shared.

Because she didn't want him to know there was a baby.

The thought of a child, *their* child, brought a strange, tight feeling to his chest. As if he were full of emotions that couldn't be contained and were bound to burst free.

Why would she leave without telling him she was pregnant? She must know he'd support her and the child. In fact, it fed right into his plan for them to marry.

Unless she had no intention of telling him about the baby.

His eyes burned as he stared at the package. His gut squeezed so hard, he felt nauseous.

He felt like he'd swallowed a knot of barbed wire.

It went against everything he thought of her—but was it possible Eva intended to get rid of the child without even letting him know she was pregnant? Did she think so little of him she imagined he wouldn't care about the baby they'd made? That he didn't deserve to be informed?

CHAPTER FOURTEEN

EVA WOKE WHEN Paul got up. Not that she'd been asleep, more dazed and spent. And not wanting to be awake enough to focus on what had just happened.

Now she couldn't avoid it.

Her mind raced like a hunted animal, scurrying here and there, hitting a dead end and running in another direction. But there was no escape. Whichever way she looked, and no matter how wonderful it had been, she'd just made a terrible, terrible mistake.

Hadn't she *known* intimacy with Paul would make it harder to leave? Hadn't she withstood temptation for weeks?

Whatever the future held she'd only get her mind round it when she was away from St Ancilla and Paul. How could she plan a career and a new life living in his shadow?

What they'd just shared had been utterly glorious. She didn't have words to describe it. Yet her weakness for him threatened to undermine logic and her need to escape.

Eva sat up and swung her legs over the side of the bed, fumbling at the edges of her robe and drawing them together. The belt had disappeared. Gingerly she stood on wobbly legs, holding the robe closed with one hand, looking for it.

She wanted to be clothed when Paul came back. Eva knew there was no escaping a discussion now. She had no hope of ejecting him from her room but she had no intention of facing him naked. She already felt too vulnerable with him.

Movement caught her eye and she turned.

Clearly Paul had such no qualms about nudity.

He stood in the bathroom doorway stark naked, watching her, making no move to cover himself.

Why should he? He was magnificent. Even in her misery Eva's heart flipped at the sight of his rangy, muscled body and charismatic features.

'You were going to leave without telling me, weren't you, Eva?' He folded his arms across his chest in a movement that accentuated the power of his upper body. Despite being sated and nervous, a fluttering started up in her abdomen like a thousand butterflies taking flight. As if every feminine hormone was hitting overload.

She shut her eyes for the briefest moment and clutched her robe between her breasts.

This had to stop. She had to resist.

When she looked again, nothing had changed, except this time she noticed the grim lines around his flat mouth and vertical furrows above his pinched eyebrows.

'If you were leaving next week there'd be no need to pack tonight. You're planning to go tomorrow.'

Eva followed his gaze to her open luggage and her heart sank.

Rather than retreat, she hiked her chin up and mirrored his stance, crossing her arms defensively.

'Yes, I'm leaving in the morning.' In just a few hours. Yet thinking of her escape only brought twisting pain. 'But I'd never leave without telling you. I was going to see you first.'

His raised eyebrows spoke of disbelief.

'I was!'

'And were you going to tell me then?'

Eva frowned. He was talking in circles. 'I just said I was going to tell you I planned to go.'

'Because you need to leave urgently?' His voice ground down low, a flat, unsettling note that vibrated discordantly.

'Well… Yes. I need to leave. I can't stay any longer.'

Because each day drew her closer and closer to him.

All of St Ancilla believed the fantasy that they loved each other and if she wasn't careful she'd start believing it too. It had taken her too long to wake up to the fact that particular fantasy was impossible. She couldn't afford to let herself slip back into daydreams.

'But you weren't going to tell me about the baby, were you?' It wasn't a question. It was an accusation. Like a shard of ice slicing the thick air between them.

Eva felt a tremor begin at the back of her skull to run all the way down, past her nape to the base of her spine. Her knees shook and she had to focus on keeping them steady enough to stand.

Belatedly she remembered the pregnancy kit in the bathroom.

Why, oh, why hadn't she packed it?

'Your silence is answer enough.' More ice. Except

the glare he sent her wasn't cold, it was flaming hot. 'What was the plan? Return to Tarentia and arrange a quiet abortion with no one the wiser? Without even telling me?'

Eva couldn't help it. Her jaw dropped, her mouth sagging open.

She tried to speak but choked on the words.

While she floundered Paul strode across the room. He stood so close he might have been about to scoop her up for a kiss. But the way he towered over her was more daunting than lover-like.

'Why, Eva? Couldn't you at least trust me with the truth after all we've been to each other?' To her amazement, his voice grew gruff, as if with emotion.

Eva blinked up at him, trying to get a fix on his mood. Anger, yes, but something else too.

'It's not like that.'

'No?' His lip curled in disbelief. 'You mean you intended to tell me about the baby after all?' He shook his head. 'Your actions tell another story, Princess.'

His tone dripped scorn and it galvanised something within her, giving her the strength she needed.

'I'm no liar.'

Except for the one great secret she'd striven so hard and so long to conceal—her love for him.

'Then why not tell me about the baby?' He stared down his supercilious nose at her.

Eva's hands found her hips, digging into slippery silk. Her heart pounded a protest that he should be so ready to judge her.

'There may not even be a baby. I didn't take the pregnancy test.'

For a second longer that scowl lasted, before turning
into a frown of puzzlement. He inhaled deeply, his chest
rising, decreasing the distance between them.

'I don't understand.'

Nor did she. Not really.

Her shoulders dropped a little as she shook her head.

'It's possible I'm pregnant. But when it came to the
point I discovered I didn't want to find out.'

'Eva?' His arms dropped to his sides, and the stern
lines folding the corners of his mouth turned into marks
of concern rather than scorn. 'If there's a baby, you
know I'll be there, don't you? It wouldn't be the end
of the world.'

She looked up into his deep-blue eyes and felt the
pull between them. If there was a baby, there'd be no
escaping this. She'd be tied to Paul always, even if they
didn't marry. What hope then of moving on with her
life?

Her head spun with the whirling tangle of thoughts.
The desire to bear his child versus the need to make
a clean break. The ache that made her want to lean
against that broad chest and surrender herself to a life
with Paul versus the need to build something positive
for herself—a life where one day she might be loved
as well as loving.

'I know you would,' she said heavily.

'And that's not enough for you?' His tone changed.
It almost sounded like hurt vying with pride.

When she didn't answer, he went on. 'I know it's
ultimately your decision whether you have a baby, but
surely I deserve to know?'

He looked so wounded, Eva wanted to reach up and

cup his cheek with her hand. But she didn't dare touch him. She knew where that could lead.

'Of course I'd tell you if I were pregnant.' She sighed, her hands leaving her hips and dropping to her sides, her shoulders slumping as defeat dragged at her. There seemed no way out of this. 'Maybe that's why I didn't want to find out the truth before I left. Because I needed to get away, have time to myself before I confronted the need to tell you.'

Eva heard Paul's sharply indrawn breath and imagined it sounded shaky. But it was probably just the tremors racing through her own body that made it seem so. She couldn't seem to stop them.

'Why, Eva? Why do you need to get away?' Gone was the angry man full of masculine pride. To her eyes, Paul looked as gutted as she felt.

Because I want you to care more than you do.

She bit her lip. There she went again, slipping back into her fantasy world. Except the jarring voice of reality wouldn't be silenced.

As if Paul could ever love you. You're a convenience to him. First for your money, then for sex, and now because he realises you can share his heavy workload.

The biting words stilled her emotional turmoil and gave her the strength to step back, putting space between them.

Time to end this for good. The truth would do that.

Eva was beyond counting the cost to her pride.

She drew a slow, shuddery breath and told him.

'I need to get away from you to save myself.' Even to her own ears that sounded melodramatic as she watched Paul's face pale.

'Save yourself? I'd *never* hurt you, Eva. You must know that.'

She lifted her hand towards him, wanting to smooth away the anguish lining his face, but made her arm drop without making contact.

'I know you wouldn't. Not intentionally. Just hear me out.'

She snagged a fortifying breath, but it didn't help, not when those indigo eyes were watching her with a mixture of disbelief and dismay.

Abruptly Eva turned and made for the window, leaning one hand on the carved surround. A breeze ruffled her hair and drifted across her face. It smelled of salt and cypress pines. She pulled the robe around her and fixed her gaze on the moonlight tinting the dark sea, gathering her courage.

In her peripheral vision she saw Paul move to the other side of the window. She sensed his impatience and his confusion.

'You'd never aim to hurt me, Paul, but you do— every day.'

He stiffened, ramrod-straight, but to his credit didn't interrupt.

'I need to get away,' she repeated, feeling the brand of truth in each word. 'Because I love you.'

Was that an indrawn breath or the distant hiss of the sea?

'Eva, I—'

'Let me finish. Please.' Now she'd started, it seemed almost easy to explain what she'd avoided sharing for so long.

'It's not that I fell for you the night we made love.'

It *had* been making love, for her at least. 'This isn't the result of some mad hormonal rush. I just wish it were.'

It would be easier to deal with.

She leaned her head against the window frame, eyes fixed on the distance. Because she didn't want to see Paul's appalled expression.

'I fell in love with you when I was fifteen, with as little thought as any teenager gives to her first crush. But for some reason I never grew out of it. I did try.' Her mouth curved in a brief, phantom smile. 'After a couple of years of long-distance yearning, I dated a few guys, kissed them, even planned to lose my virginity to one of them.'

Beside her Paul moved abruptly, straightening, seeming to grow taller, but Eva kept her eyes on the sea, glistening like molten silver.

'But it never went far. I always pulled away because it didn't feel right. Because I had my heart set on you.' She shook her head. 'You have no idea how thrilled I was when my parents asked if I'd be happy to marry you. It was like a dream come true.' She paused. 'Except, when we came here to celebrate the betrothal you were so wooden and cold. It was obvious even to me that you'd agreed out of duty. You barely even looked at me, much less smiled the way you used to.'

'Is that why you wouldn't let me kiss you?'

She swung round, feeling the hurt and anger well up in her throat despite her determination to stay calm. 'What did you expect? I knew you had a reputation as a bit of a playboy, and that women flocked to you, but you didn't even attempt to talk with me, not properly. You just expected me to kiss you because we'd signed a contract. As if you'd bought me with a signature on a piece of parchment!' That still hurt.

'That's not true! I didn't really know you.' He shook his head. 'My father made it clear you were a dutiful daughter, doing what her family expected. I was trying to do what was expected of me too, but you barely looked at me—'

'Because I was *shy* and petrified you'd discover how I felt. Especially when I discovered how uninterested you were. Everywhere we went there were beautiful women ogling you, vying for your attention, yet you were stuck with me.'

Paul was clearly about to interrupt so she hurried on.

'It doesn't matter. What does matter is that I spent the next four years preparing as best I could to be your wife, doing the degree my parents approved of, but on the side learning Ancillan and everything I could about your country. I was convinced that once we were married and you saw how good a wife I was you'd fall for me.' Her throat closed on the words and she had to swallow a knot of burning emotion.

She waved a dismissive hand. 'But I saw my mistake last month when you rejected me. I realised nothing I ever did would change how you felt. That's when I discovered I didn't want to waste my life with a man who didn't love me. I want to be appreciated, desired, loved for myself.'

'Is that why you went to the night club—looking for someone who desired you?' She couldn't read Paul's tone and his expression gave nothing away.

She shrugged. 'It turns out I'm not into casual hookups, which is why I decided to leave so early.'

And then it all went wrong.

Eva drew her robe closer around her. 'The details don't matter. What's important is that I've grown up. I'm no longer the little innocent who turned you into her Prince Charming.'

That was only half a lie. Eva still thought him the most appealing man she'd ever met, but she saw him as he was. Honest and hard working but prone to shoulder too much. Decisive and inclined to take charge. Sexy and gentle and…

'For my own good I need to leave because I don't want to be married to you, Paul. It would be emotional suicide. That's why I don't want to know yet if I'm pregnant. Because I need some space and time before I face that possibility.'

Admitting it should have made Eva feel weak but instead pride rose. She could do this, despite the gnawing grief at the thought of leaving.

'Because you couldn't bear it if we've made a baby together?' His voice ground low and harsh.

'I don't…' Eva floundered, caught between fear of the implications and heady joy at the idea.

'Because you can't bear to be near me.'

'Can't you see, Paul? Every day we're together it eats away at me—this pretence that I'm special to you, that you care.'

'I *do* care.' Sparkling eyes snared hers but she fought their terrible pull.

'Of course you care. You're a decent man. But you don't love me. And that's what I want. A man who loves *me*.'

For a long, long moment he stood, unmoving, looking down at her from his superior height, his expression unreadable.

'That night I tried to kiss you, the night of our betrothal ball, it wasn't what you thought.'

Of all the things he might have said that was the least expected. Why wasn't Paul agreeing that it was time she left? Why rehash the past?

'My father had a word with me after our betrothal.' Paul's mouth quirked up at one side but she read no amusement in that lop-sided smile. 'Too late, he told me I shouldn't assume you *wanted* to marry me. He mentioned you'd been seen with a handsome young count in Tarentia. But that you'd been made to give him up to do your duty and marry me.'

Eva's head jerked up. She knew who he was talking about. She'd gone on a date with the count, had kissed him, and thought about doing much more with him, to cure herself of her infatuation with Paul. But when it came to the crunch she'd shied away.

Paul spread his hands. 'I was a young man with a young man's pride, so perhaps I didn't handle it well, but I had to know how you felt about me.'

'That's why you offered to kiss me?'

He inclined his head. 'When you declined and looked at me with that frozen stare I knew you didn't really want to marry me. I decided then and there to set you free.'

Eva stared, amazed at this new explanation for the excruciating scene she remembered.

'I told my father I was calling off the engagement.' Paul's expression turned grim. 'That's when he informed me he'd already spent the portion of your dowry that was handed over on our engagement. I had no way of paying that back so no way of releasing you.'

Eva stared, realising how well that explained his distance, always polite but never anything more than that.

'Thank you for telling me.' The truth made it better somehow. 'But you didn't love me then and you don't now.' She was proud of the fact her words sounded even, almost crisp. 'So it's better that I leave.'

Warm fingers folded around hers and Eva looked down to see his strong hand cradling hers. The sight made her heartbeat blip and her breath hitch.

'No, I didn't love you, Eva.'

Her breath released in a silent sigh. The truth shouldn't hurt. She'd known it so long she should be used to it. Yet the pain was there, the ever-present ache behind her ribs.

'But I do now.'

'Sorry?' She swung her head up to meet eyes of heart-stopping blue and an expression that made her insides dance. He wasn't smiling. If anything, Paul looked grave.

'I love you, Eva.'

She tugged her hand but his grip held. So did that stunning, bright gaze, like lapis lazuli.

'Don't, Paul. You don't have to pretend. I'll tell you if there's a baby, I promise.'

'This has nothing to do with whether or not you're pregnant.'

Her heart stuttered then took up a chaotic rhythm.

'I love you. That's why I don't want you to go. Because I want to marry you and spend the rest of our days together.'

Her lips trembled. Eva realised her control was crumbling. Any minute now there'd be tears, for this was too much. She blinked and straightened her crumpled mouth.

'You want someone to share your burdens, that's all. But believe me, Paul, there'll be women lining up to the other side of the island once they know you're single again.'

'I don't want any woman but you.'

She opened her mouth but her words died when he pressed his finger to her lips.

'When you came to St Ancilla this time, I'd resolved to end the betrothal. But, when it came to it, I was strangely unsettled. I knew it was the honourable thing to do, but it didn't sit right and I didn't know why. Later that night, I discovered why.' He drew a deep breath that expanded his chest hugely. 'I wanted you, Eva. I'd never known anything like it—desire so brutally potent it cut through every scruple, every good intention to keep my distance.'

Heat licked Eva's veins. She knew exactly what he meant. It had been like that for her too. It still was.

Stiffly she shrugged. 'Lust. That's all.'

His head swung from side to side. 'Don't downplay it, Eva. I've never felt anything so powerful in my life. Well, except for once.'

She didn't want to hear this. Surely he wasn't going to tell her about some other woman? She cringed.

'It was the same night. When I saw that guy groping you, threatening you.' Paul's mouth twisted. 'I felt a roar of rage so powerful, I couldn't control myself. The idea of him touching you... I couldn't bear it. I'd have acted no matter who you were, but that fury was because he hurt *you*.' He hesitated. 'And because you're mine.'

Eva blinked, thrown off-balance by his words. 'Officially yours, because of the betrothal agreement, but not really yours. Not in ways that matter.'

He was playing with her emotions and she didn't think she could bear it.

'That's what I used to think. But that night it made no difference. I always counted myself a civilised man, Eva, but that night, once I got my hands on him, I didn't want to stop.'

Stunned, she stared up at him, seeing something in Paul's face she'd never seen before.

'I told myself it was the heat of the moment. And later that it was just sex and four years' abstinence that made our night together seem remarkable. But my feelings for you didn't dim. They grew. I watch you with my people and you're wonderful. I look forward to the time we spend together every day. I value your opinions. I admire your courage and determination. I *care* about you, Eva.'

'I know you do, Paul, but that's not love.'

Why wouldn't he just let her *go*? This was torture.

He reached for her other hand, grasping them both tightly, as if willing her to understand.

'I'm trying to sound reasonable, Eva. Because what I feel doesn't seem reasonable at all. My heart thuds faster when you're around. Or even when I think of you. When you smile at me, my heart squeezes so tight, sometimes I can't breathe. I think of you all the time, imagining what you're doing, wondering how I can make you smile, make you stay with me. The thought of you leaving scares me.'

He ground to a halt and to her amazement Eva realised his breath had turned ragged and there was a pulse beating frantically at his temple. As if he was in true distress.

What he described was so familiar. And the look on his face…

'Paul, you—'

'Please, Eva. It's my turn. Let me tell you.'

He waited and, torn between hope and disbelief, she nodded, her heart racing dangerously fast.

Paul squeezed her fingers, his eyes never leaving hers. She shivered from her scalp to her toes, rocked by the profundity of that stare. She'd never seen him look so serious, or so determined.

'I want to share my life with you, Eva—not because you're a perfect princess who'll do me proud, but because I can't imagine not having you by my side.'

He swallowed and her gaze tracked the jerky movement, reading his tension. Eva dragged in a sharp, sustaining breath that burned in her tight lungs.

'I want to have children with you and raise them together. Not as I was raised, but in a loving, warm family.' His searing gaze held hers and she could almost swear she heard sparks sizzle. 'Or, if we can't have children, then we'll make a wonderful aunt and uncle team for our nephews and nieces.'

'Oh, Paul.' Her throat was so clogged, the words were a whisper she doubted he heard.

He was turning her inside out.

'I want to grow old with you, Eva. Though not just

yet. There are too many things I want to enjoy with you before we reach old age.' Paul lifted first one hand then the other to his lips, kissing her knuckles, sending flutters of delight through her.

'I can't tell you the exact moment I fell in love with you, darling, but I can tell you I will always love you.'

He sighed, then breathed in deeply while Eva still struggled for breath. What he said, the way he said it, was unlike anything she'd ever imagined. Far better than any fantasy. For this was *real*. So real and raw, it came close to pain.

'Are you going to say something?'

His voice was the same, strong and deep, but she didn't miss the hint of a tremor. Eva felt it too in the powerful hands grasping hers.

She freed one hand, saw him frown as she did so then planted her palm on his wide chest. There it was again—a tremor. His heart beat strongly but unevenly. Its rhythm matched hers, too quick and hard for comfort.

Slowly Eva smiled, the radiance of love given and returned unfurling within her. She watched him see it and his own mouth curved up into a grin so wide, she felt it brand her with its brilliance.

'I say *yes*. Please.'

They had so much to talk about, so much to share. But that would wait. It had to, for suddenly his arms were around her, her hands were grabbing his shoulders and they were kissing with all the passion, longing and triumph of lovers who'd finally, against the odds, found each other. Lovers secure in the knowledge that this was the beginning of their very own happily-ever-after.

EPILOGUE

As THEY WALTZED together at his birthday ball, around
them whirled a multitude of guests, some from his
wife's homeland of Tarentia, some from further afield—
like his half-sister Caro and her husband Jake, who lived
mainly in Sydney. Though most guests in the gilded
ballroom came from St Ancilla.

It warmed Paul's heart, the way his people had welcomed Eva, and the way she'd responded with true
generosity of spirit. On the day of their wedding, nine
months ago, there'd been no whisper in his country of
disquiet or innuendo about his bride, no raking up of
scandalous old gossip.

His people loved her almost as much as he did.

His heart lurched as he looked down at her, slim and
smiling in his arms, her off-the-shoulder dress of aqua-
marine a perfect match for her favourite tiara.

The enormity of his feelings hit him and he hesitated
a second longer than optimal on a turn. Instantly bright
silvery eyes snared his. His heart gave a mighty thump.
They were so attuned, he still found it hard to believe.

'Paul?'

The music ended and he raised Eva's fingers to his

lips. He didn't dare kiss her on the lips, as he'd learned that even a crowd of onlookers couldn't stop him wanting more when he tasted her mouth.

She really was the most special woman.

Suddenly it was imperative that he tell her so. Putting her arm in his, he led them through the glamorous crowd, nodding and chatting briefly as they passed, but never stopping.

Caro, vibrant with her red hair, jade-green dress and glorious smile, caught his eye from one side of the room. She waved a beckoning hand to where she stood with Jake and another couple, Eva's brother Leo and a woman he didn't recognise.

Soon, he mouthed to his sister. He had something vital to do before mingling with guests.

'Is anything wrong?' Eva asked under her breath as his pace quickened.

'No, nothing wrong.'

He pressed her hand as they approached wide French doors guarded by a staff member in formal dress. Moments later they were on a private terrace looking out over the royal gardens. From around the corner came the sound of voices where guests took in the views.

The door closed and Paul turned to his wife.

'You're beautiful,' he breathed, his gaze fixed on her shining eyes.

'Thank you.' Her smile grew impish. 'You brush up well yourself, Your Handsomeness. Half the women in there are in love with you, but you're mine, and I'm not letting you go.'

'Excellent.' He lashed his arms around her. 'As for

other women, I didn't notice them. I was too busy warning off the men salivating at the sight of you.'

Eva shook her head as if she didn't believe him, but it was true. Love made him possessive. It was a good thing he trusted his wife totally.

'Why are we here?'

His mouth curved in a private smile. 'Because I need to kiss you, my sweet, and tell you how much I love you.'

Eva looped her hands around his neck, a siren smile curving her lips. 'Wonderful. I was just thinking the same thing. I love you too, Paul, so very much.'

Grinning now, he lowered his head, only to pause when she put her finger to his lips.

'Since we're here to talk about important things…'

'Yes?' Impatience stirred. It had been hours since he'd kissed her.

'I have something to tell you too. A birthday surprise.'

He nodded. Hard to believe it had been a whole year since the extraordinary night he and Eva had confronted their feelings for each other.

'You know I love surprises.' He glanced around them. 'Though perhaps with a little more privacy.'

His wife shook her head with an attempt at prim censure that didn't reach her eyes. Then her expression turned serious. She reached round and grabbed one of his hands. A moment later it rested on her belly. Instantly his fingers splayed wide. He loved touching Eva, even through her dress…

'We're going to have a baby.'

He gaped down at her. 'We are?'

It had turned out that early pregnancy scare was a false alarm. He hadn't minded. He'd been happy to have Eva all to himself, though lately he'd thought she fretted a little whenever her period arrived. 'Are you happy?' he asked.

She nodded but her eyes looked huge as she surveyed him. As if waiting for his response.

'Good,' he growled, feeling a whole host of emotions slam into him. Delight, pride, excitement and not a little fear.

Paul tilted her chin up with a hand that was just a fraction unsteady, all the while holding her gaze.

'I didn't think anything could come near the joy of hearing that you love me. And now you give me this.' He pressed a gentle, almost reverent kiss to her lips. 'I don't know how I can ever give you anything to make you as happy as I am now.'

Her mouth eased into a wide smile as she threaded her fingers through the hair at the back of his skull.

'You don't have to do anything, Paul. Just keep loving me the way you do.'

'Always, my darling.' He pulled her close for a kiss that was as tender as it was passionate, and Paul, King of St Ancilla, knew without doubt that he was the luckiest, happiest man on the planet.

* * * * *

#3881 THE GREEK'S CONVENIENT CINDERELLA
by Lynne Graham

Jude would be lying if he said he hadn't imagined the passion he might share with innocent Tansy—his bride of pure convenience. But he didn't plan for his tempting Cinderella to make him rethink the world as he sees it...

#3882 RETURNING TO CLAIM HIS HEIR
The Avelar Family Scandals
by Amanda Cinelli

Nora never expected to see Duarte again. She thought he was dead! Worse still, he has no idea who she is! Now she must quell her addictive feelings for him, because she knows everything will change when she reveals that her newborn son is Duarte's heir...

#3883 WAKING UP IN HIS ROYAL BED
by Kim Lawrence

Waking up next to her soon-to-be-ex husband, Crown Prince Dante, Beatrice is determined this will be their *final* goodbye. Despite their ever-present chemistry, she's done with a life of royal scrutiny. Until a positive pregnancy test makes walking away impossible...

#3884 INNOCENT'S DESERT WEDDING CONTRACT
by Heidi Rice

Sheikh Karim needs a wife in order to avoid his father's royal retribution. Orla Calhoun needs to save her family's stud farm. The no-sex clause of their contract should make things simple...if they can contain their simmering chemistry!

#3885 AFTER THE BILLIONAIRE'S WEDDING VOWS...
by Lucy Monroe

Greek tycoon Andros's whirlwind romance with Polly started white-hot. Five years later, the walls he's built threaten to push her away forever! With his marriage on the line, Andros must win back his wife. Their passion still burns bright, but can it break down their barriers?

#3886 FORBIDDEN HAWAIIAN NIGHTS
Secrets of the Stowe Family
by Cathy Williams

Max Stowe is commanding and completely off-limits as Mia Kaiwi's temporary boss! But there's no escape from temptation working so closely together... Dare she explore their connection for a few scorching nights?

#3887 THE PLAYBOY PRINCE OF SCANDAL
The Acostas!
by Susan Stephens

Prince Cesar will never forgive polo star Sofia Acosta for the article branding him a playboy! But to avoid further scandal he must invite her to his lavish banquet in Rome. Where he's confronted by her unexpected apology and their *very* obvious electricity!

#3888 THE MAN SHE SHOULD HAVE MARRIED
by Louise Fuller

Famed movie director Farlan has come a long way from the penniless boy whose ring Nia rejected. But their surprise reunion proves there's one thing he'll never be able to relinquish...their dangerously electric connection!

YOU CAN FIND MORE INFORMATION ON UPCOMING HARLEQUIN TITLES, FREE EXCERPTS AND MORE AT HARLEQUIN.COM.

HPCNMRB0121

"Mr. Alexandris," Tansy pronounced rather stiffly.

"Come sit down," he invited lazily. "Tea or coffee?"

"Coffee please," Tansy said, following him around a sectional room divider into a rather more intimate space furnished with sumptuous sofas and then sinking down into the comfortable depths of one, her tense spine rigorously protesting that amount of relaxation.

She was fighting to get a grip on her composure again but nothing about Jude Alexandris in the flesh matched the formal online images she had viewed. He wasn't wearing a sharply cut business suit—he was wearing faded, ripped and worn jeans that outlined long, powerful thighs and narrow hips and accentuated the prowling natural grace of his every movement. An equally casual dark gray cotton top complemented the jeans. One sleeve was partially pushed up to reveal a strong brown forearm and a small tattoo that appeared to be printed letters of some sort. His garb reminded her that although he might be older than her, he was still only in his late twenties, and that unlike her, he had felt no need to dress to impress.

Her pride stung at the knowledge that she was little more than a commodity on Alexandris's terms. Either he would choose her or he wouldn't. She had put herself on the market to be bought, though, she thought with sudden self-loathing. How could she blame Jude Alexandris for her stepfather's use of virtual blackmail to get her agreement? Everything she was doing was for Posy, she reminded herself squarely, and the end would justify the means…wouldn't it?

"So…" Tansy remarked in a stilted tone because she was determined not to sit there acting like the powerless person she knew herself to be in his presence. "You require a fake wife…"

HPEXP0121

Jude shifted a broad shoulder in a very slight shrug. "Only we would know it was fake. It would have to seem real to everyone else from the start to the very end," he advanced calmly. "Everything between us would have to remain confidential."

"I'm not a gossip, Mr. Alexandris." In fact, Tansy almost laughed at the idea of even having anyone close enough to confide in, because she had left her friends behind at university, and certainly none of them had seemed to understand her decision to make herself responsible for her baby sister rather than return to the freedom of student life.

"I trust no one," Jude countered without apology. "You would be legally required to sign a nondisclosure agreement before I married you."

"Understood. My stepfather explained that to me," Tansy acknowledged, her attention reluctantly drawn to his careless sprawl on the sofa opposite, the long, muscular line of a masculine thigh straining against well-washed denim. Her head tipped back, her color rising as she made herself look at his face instead, encountering glittering dark eyes that made the breath hitch in her throat.

"I find you attractive, too," Jude Alexandris murmured as though she had spoken.

"I don't know what you're talking about," Tansy protested, the faint pink in her cheeks heating exponentially. Her stomach flipped while she wondered if she truly could be read that easily by a man.

"For this to work, we would need that physical attraction. Nobody is likely to be fooled by two strangers pretending what they don't feel, least of all my family, some of whom are shrewd judges of character."

Tansy had paled. "Why would we need attraction? I assumed this was to be a marriage on paper, nothing more."

"Then you assumed wrong," Jude told her without skipping a beat.

Don't miss
The Greek's Convenient Cinderella
available February 2021 wherever
Harlequin Presents books and ebooks are sold.

Harlequin.com

Love Harlequin romance?

DISCOVER.

Be the first to find out about promotions, news and exclusive content!

Facebook.com/HarlequinBooks

Twitter.com/HarlequinBooks

Instagram.com/HarlequinBooks

Pinterest.com/HarlequinBooks

ReaderService.com

EXPLORE.

Sign up for the Harlequin e-newsletter and download a free book from any series at **TryHarlequin.com**

CONNECT.

Join our Harlequin community to share your thoughts and connect with other romance readers!
Facebook.com/groups/HarlequinConnection